ISLAND

Island

Alice Renton

First published in Great Britain in 2023 by Flint Cottage Editions

Edited, designed and produced by Tandem Publishing
http://tandempublishing.yolasite.com

Cover design by Alice Carter: https://alicecarterartist.com

ISBN: 9798395329431

10 9 8 7 6 5 4 3 2 1

A CIP catalogue record for this book is available from the British Library.

For my family

Also by Alice Renton

Victoria: Biography of a Pigeon

Maiden Speech

Winter Butterfly

Tyrant or Victim? A History of the British Governess

The island in these stories is not an island I know. These are people I never met or heard of. But the ideas, I acknowledge, come from many years of visiting an island that I know a little, and where I feel at home.

DUNES

BAIDEANACH

Morag McEachern's
house

Donald etni's
house

McRae's croft

BALINBEAG

School

Neil's house

CEAN BODHA

DUNES

Miss MacFarlane's
guest house

Bessie's h
(now a ru

paved road ———
unpaved road ------

THE ISLAND

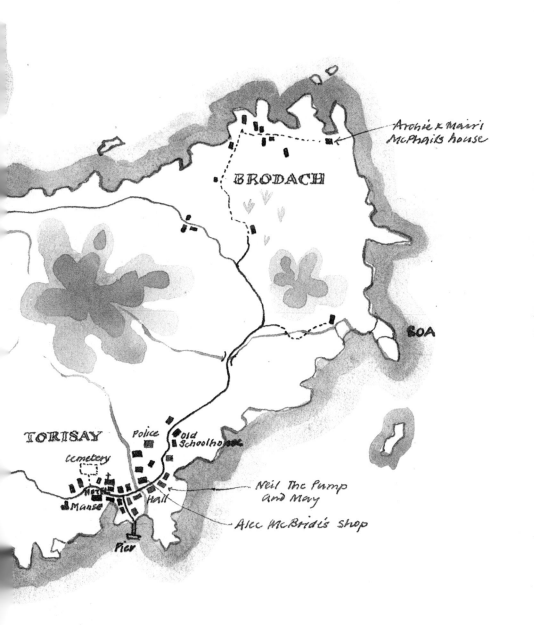

Archie & Mairi McPhail's house

BRODACH

BOA

TORISAY

Police

Old Schoolhouse

Cemetery

Hotel

Manse

Hall

Pier

Neil The Pump and Mary

Alec McBride's shop

Contents

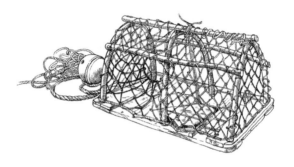

JOHN DONALD

1950s

John Donald MacQueen was an essentially private man. Privacy was so important to him that many of his actions were dictated solely by his need for it. Nor would he ever think of invading the privacy of others by asking any questions more intrusive than as to a neighbour's health; and he would do that by way of a statement – 'You're keeping well, then.' Any answer more informative than the routine, 'Not so bad, thanks,' would make him recoil within himself and wish that he had not been so bold.

The endemic reticence of the people of the Hebrides can be mistaken for dourness; but it is, rather, a natural restraint arising from a deeply rooted sense of good manners, and it very often conceals warm and hospitable hearts. But the reticence of John Donald was a by-word even among these people. They said his grandfather, who had been his close companion since an early age, had been just the same.

The grandfather had been known as John Donald Sòa, this being the small tidal island off the beach in front of his croft house. The

name distinguished him from all the other John Donald Mac-
Queens who lived in the neighbourhood. The islanders were not
so much unimaginative as bound by tradition in the naming of
their offspring, and to name a first-born son after his grandfather
was normal and expected. As a child the young John Donald had
been referred to as John Donald Beag, little John Donald, but,
since the old man's death ten years earlier, people in the neighbourhood had begun to refer to him, too, as John Donald Sòa.

He signed his name in full, now, in his pension book, and
pushed it across the counter. The girl, who didn't look old enough
to be out of school, banged the rubber stamp down on it, back to
the ink pad and down again.

John Donald's weekly visit to the post office in Torisay was an
ordeal. He needed the money, for his croft was small and lamb
prices had been poor for the last two years. But the public act
of obtaining it was something he dreaded. It had nothing to do
with revealing his age to the lassie behind the counter, or with
her knowing how much money he was collecting. It was being
looked at, thought about, talked to at close quarters by another
individual that he found so deeply embarrassing. With a man
behind the grill it would have been bad enough.

'Will you be needing stamps this week, John Donald?' asked
the girl, cockily. She looked at the elderly tweed cap bent over the
counter in front of her. It was seldom you got a good look at John
Donald's face. If he had to wait while someone else was being
served, he would stand with his back turned, his hands deep in
the pockets of his overalls, studying intently the small posters
on the wall, the advice for applying for grants and subsidies. He
would turn round only when his turn came. Then you saw a
square, friendly face, not plump nor lean, with no particularly
unusual features, a blue-eyed, elderly, tanned face, lined by age
and weather. It had never been what you would call handsome,
but it was certainly not a face that needed hiding.

'Stamps, John Donald. First class? Second class?'

She only said it to tease: if John Donald ever posted a letter no one knew about it.

'No. No thanks,' he muttered, keeping his eyes down as he slid the loose coins into his palm. He stuffed them on top of the notes in his pocket, to be sorted out quietly later.

He did his weekly shopping in Alec MacBride's store quickly and furtively, asking for his needs in a low voice, but usually doing without anything he could not see for himself on the shelves.

As he bicycled away up the single-track road to his croft, three or more miles gently rising and falling over small rocky hills and patches of drained grazing land, he felt his spirits lifting. Soon he began to whistle.

His thoughts went to his grandfather as they often did, almost as if for companionship.

'Keep yourself to yourself and there's no one will bother you,' was what the old man used to say; and he had never found reason to disregard this advice, which fell in with his natural inclinations.

John Donald's father had died in 1899, drowned while serving in the Merchant Navy. His mother had taken the same road some years earlier while giving birth to his only sibling, a stillborn sister. So the two John Donalds, grandfather and grandson, had kept each other company for nigh on forty-five years, and very little had the rest of the island seen of them during that time. The odd funeral, the sheep sales, church on Sunday, but few other events brought them out in public.

The early years, when the boy had walked nearly four miles each way daily to school, had not been happy ones. The chores he was required to do on the croft meant that he had no time for play after school, so he made few friends. He was teased by the boys for his unwillingness to fight, and he was mocked by the girls for his shyness and the pink flush that rose readily to his face. He found it almost impossible to answer questions when the attention of the whole class was focused on him, and he gained a reputation for being a little slow, which he did not deserve.

At fourteen with great relief he threw his school satchel on to the dump and stayed at home to learn the things that were going to be important to him, ways of gleaning a living from the land and from the sea. There was nothing his grandfather could not teach him about those.

Old John Donald Sōa, after ninety-nine and a half years of almost perfect health, died suddenly one night out of fear (it was rumoured at the hotel bar) that someone might tell the Queen when he reached his century. If John Donald mourned, he did not look for solace in his grief, and the pattern of his life during the years that followed did not change. He kept himself to himself. His grandfather's other stricture, 'Do not have anything to do with women folk, for they will only bring you trouble,' he also observed.

The tarmac petered out at the edge of his croft, and he pushed his bicycle for the last three quarters of a mile. He had never seen any point in laying a hard-core track over his land, as the other crofters did. It was expensive and only encouraged trippers who liked to find remote spots for their picnics. It was easy enough to follow the sheep tracks between the low rocks, and he knew the ground so well that he could do it as easily by night as by day.

As he came over the slight rise behind his home, John Donald stood, leaning his stocky frame for a moment on his bicycle, surveying with searching eyes the scene before him. All seemed as he had left it, the small whitewashed croft house stood at the head of the narrow bay, well above the highest point of the winter 'spring' tides, but still close to the shore. His boat, that he and his grandfather had built together, was on a running mooring halfway out into the bay where it would not go dry as the tide ebbed in the evening.

At low water he would go out and lift his lobster creels, the greatest pleasure of his day, and he would have a good two hours before sunset. He pushed his bicycle into the lean-to shed at the end of the house, unloaded his shopping, and went round to the front.

The total unexpectedness of what he saw made him gasp: a woman, a completely strange woman, was sitting on the bench under his kitchen window.

John Donald's first instinct was to get away quickly, to give himself time to think about this horror and how to deal with it; but before he could summon his limbs into activity the woman turned her head and saw him.

'Hello,' she said, as if to be sitting there was the most normal thing in the world. She was young, he could see that.

He was unable to answer, but she continued, rising to her feet.

'Are you Mr MacQueen? My name is Jane Parker. Please excuse me for walking in on you like this. I'm just visiting the island, staying at the hotel in Torisay. I was told how lovely your little bay is here, so I came over to see for myself. I do hope you don't mind. I knocked on the door, actually, but as you were out I thought I would sit down and enjoy the view.'

His shock at the intrusion still showed in his face, for she said then:

'I know I am disturbing you, and I expect you are busy. Don't worry, I'm off now. I must get back to the village before supper time. See you again, I hope.'

Her voice was bright and quick, her accent English, and he was still absorbing the meaning of her words when she was already waving a hand from halfway up the rocks.

John Donald released his two collies from the shed in which they had been shut during this absence, then, back in his kitchen, went mechanically through the motions of unpacking his shopping bags. His hands were steady, but his mind was trembling.

The dogs followed him round to the steadings and lay with their chins on their paws watching him as he replaced the broken hinges on the byre door. Later, he went down to the shore, and they sat on the beach awaiting his return.

Normally, taking his boat out on a perfect June evening like this was a soothing experience, and John Donald would have fished for a while after lifting his creels. But tonight he was troubled. He did no fishing; it was early in the season yet, for lobsters, and several of his creels needed no rebaiting; so he was home earlier than usual, in no mood for trawling for saithe in the dying light of the sun.

He sat late in front of his small fire of coal and driftwood, a mug of tea between his hands and his mind on the implications of his visitor's parting words. 'See you again, I hope…' Was she just being polite, or did she mean to turn up again, uninvited? He felt invaded and vulnerable, and had no idea what he could do to protect himself. His home no longer felt like a safe haven.

The next day, after seeing to the sheep, he decided to go for the creels in mid-afternoon, so if by chance 'that woman', as he referred to her in his mind, reappeared he would be well out of the way.

Three hours later as he nosed his boat round the rocks at the entrance of the bay, the out-board motor throttled well down, he could see the bench at the front of his house was unoccupied. With some relief he speeded up and came in confidently to where his lobster keep was moored. This was a floating wooden cage made from two wooden fish boxes nailed together; it rose and fell with the tide, always half under water.

He untied the lid and slid under it the day's catch of five mottled blue lobsters, their claws securely tied like those of the other captives inside. When he had collected forty or fifty he would pack them up and send them off to the mainland by the ferry boat that called three times a week. Eventually they would appear on restaurant tables in England and France at ten times the price he was paid by the local dealer.

He moved the boat over to his mooring and cut the engine, heaving it up to a safe overnight angle. It was as he was securing the ends of the running mooring rope to the bow and stern rings that he heard the voice, and his heart plunged.

'I see you caught some lobsters – that's fantastic!'

John Donald Sōa kept his head down and finished his knots before looking up. She was standing on the rocks just where he must bring his boat in. Worse still, she had a camera in her hand. He turned his head away as he pulled the boat hand over hand along the rope till it gently bumped the rock. She was down by the edge of the water now, reaching for the prow. The camera had disappeared.

'Can I give you a hand? I'm not too bad with boats.'

She was wearing jeans, a heavy jersey and sensible rubber boots with heavily rutted soles. She was younger than he remembered, a girl, really, but not a school-girl. Older than that. She was pale, like a tripper, with dark hair tied back out of the way.

Efficiently, she held the boat in while he climbed onto the rock, and then she gave it a push out into the bay. John Donald pulled on the rope until the boat was nearly out at the mooring, and then tied the loose end on to the ring cemented into the rock above the high-tide mark.

'Thank you,' he said then. After considering it, he had decided he could say no less.

Before he could stop her, she had lifted the black plastic bucket in which silver blue saithe slithered upon each other with gaping mouths and slit bellies.

'I'll give you a hand to the house, shall I?' she said, and set off across the rocks.

John Donald sighed. He felt completely out of control. He picked up his oilskin and petrol can and followed her. Despite his fears, she did not linger, beyond telling him what a perfect day it had been, and adding: 'I've hired a car from Mr MacBride, I think his name is, at the store, so I can see more of the island. I've left it up on the road.'

And then she left.

A car. There was nothing to stop her turning up every day, then. John Donald was swept by a sense of foreboding, and then pulled himself together.

'It's only a lassie. What harm can she do me?'

He heard the echo of his grandfather's voice: 'Women ... they will only bring you trouble.' Often when he had a problem he would turn his mind to the old man and ask himself what advice he would have given. It was comforting of an evening to imagine old John Donald Sòa sitting across the hearth from him, smoking his pipe, talking quietly or reading aloud from the Old Testament, as he had for so many years. Sometimes if he felt tempted to take an unwise short-cut, say in the anchoring of a haystack or the tarring of a roof, he would sense the familiar presence reminding, chiding, and ruefully he would agree, and do the job the way he had been taught. But he was at a loss as to what his grandfather would have advised in the present situation.

The next day, in the unpredictable way of Hebridean weather, strong south-easterly wind gusted over the island and the sea broke up into white-capped peaks, too treacherous for a clinker-built dinghy with a small Seagull outboard engine. John Donald realised that by staying ashore he was laying himself open to attack, but he was not going to let himself be driven into danger by this possibility. His respect for the sea was unreserved, based on experience. He knew this dark, sun-bright water was not for him.

He spent most of the morning at the sheep, a mixed bunch of blackface crosses whose independent nature caused them to scatter far and wide in search of grazing. In doing his daily count he could have sent his two collies to search for them, but he preferred to find out for himself where his flock was wandering; they sometimes strayed on to grassy ledges down the low cliffs by the water, and he had known the sudden appearance of a dog to startle a ewe over the edge. This way, too, he could feel he knew what was going on over every inch of his territory.

By mid-afternoon he was sitting on his low bench, a roll of twine and a knife beside him, mending the netting of some of last season's creels. He used a worn and shiny wooden 'needle' his grandfather had made and taught him to use when he was just a lad. But though he concentrated on his work, the same mood was on him that he felt before a visit to the island doctor, when he would have to reveal private things about himself. Such was his tension that he felt a positive sense of relief when the shadow fell over his hands from the right. She should know, he thought, it was bad manners to approach a man's house with the sun at your back.

'Hello, Mr MacQueen.' Her voice was gentler, less brisk today. 'It's a wonderful day, but too rough for you to go out in the boat, I suppose?'

'That is so,' he replied, his eyes still on his work.

'May I watch you for a little?'

She did not wait for him to answer but sat down a short way from him along the bench. This was a long driftwood plank, propped up on wooden fish boxes. She was silent for a while, and he felt his hands grow clumsy.

'Do you make your own lobster pots?' she said.

'I do.'

Another pause.

'What kind of wood do you use for those bent bits?'

John Donald looked at the arches, made to support the netting, which he had steamed into shape over his kettle during winter evenings.

'It is hazel.'

'But not from the island, surely? I haven't seen any trees at all.'

A pause again.

'No,' he said. 'No, there are no trees on the island.'

'No. Why is that?'

'The soil is very shallow over the rock. And with the wind we get here in winter a tree would never get a hold.'

'So you have to get the hazel from the mainland?'

'I do. There is no wood at all to be had on the island, unless what the sea brings in.'

Jane listened in fascination to the carefully enunciated words. She knew the older islanders had spoken only Gaelic in their homes when they were children and had learnt English at school almost as a foreign language. The soft Highland accent was not new to her, but it never failed to give her pleasure. She tried to keep the conversation going, but as if alarmed at the amount he had already said, John Donald relapsed into shy 'I am's', and 'I do's' in reply to her questioning.

Feeling she had made some progress she did not push her luck by staying too long. When he rose to his feet, rolling up the ball of twine, she stood up too, and said: 'I must be off. Would you mind if I dropped in again, when I am passing? I really love this end of the island, especially your bay.'

'There is no law of trespass in Scotland,' he said. It was a phrase he had once heard his grandfather use to a hiker.

Jane was not dissatisfied. From anyone else the comment would have been a snub, she thought, but John Donald's manner was so courteous it gave no offence.

In the following days Jane Parker played John Donald Sōa like a fish on a light line. She approached him quietly, springing no verbal surprises, making no sudden movements, and always withdrawing tactically if she became aware of any tension in his manner. Thinking back to the first days she knew he was gradually relaxing and coming to accept her frequent presence. It gave her great satisfaction to remember they had told her in the village that she would never get near him. She was proving them wrong.

Changing her pattern, she arrived fairly early one morning, and since he made no objection she walked out with him to check the sheep. It was a still day, and a thin drift of rain had given a moist softness to the air; the waves rolled quietly along the rocks and even the cry of the oystercatchers on the shore was muted.

She watched, intrigued, as the dogs cornered a lame ewe in a gully so John Donald could trim and treat an infected foot. Strong hands, she noted, a doctor's hands, gentle but very firm. She enjoyed his relationship with his dogs; there was no sentimentality there, they were working companions who were briefly scolded when they did wrong and needed no praise when they did their job correctly. She never saw John Donald fondle them; their devotion did not seem to depend on any physical contact. He appeared rather to stroke them with his look, and when they were nearby the collies' eyes were always on his face. A perfect partnership – the words seemed apt.

Watching him mend a fence on another day, Jane said to him: 'They tell me you are known as John Donald Sōa.'

She gave it the Gaelic pronunciation – So-ay.

John Donald blenched inwardly at the thought that she had been discussing him in the village. He hit a staple twice with his hammer before replying.

'Yes,' he said. 'My grandfather was called the same.'

'Did he live here too?'

'He did.'

'You were very fond of your grandfather?'

John Donald took this as a statement and, leaning for a moment on a fence post, pondered it, gazing at the horizon with unfocused eyes. Defiantly, he decided he could talk about his grandfather if he wanted.

'He was a good man,' he said then. 'He taught me all I know.'

Jane felt she was on sensitive ground and moved accordingly.

'I know so little,' she said, 'about the things you know. Animals and birds and things. I saw a really amazing duck on the beach as I came along this morning, white and brown and black and green, I think. It didn't look real, more like a child's toy, carved out of wood and painted.'

'That would be a shelduck,' he said, without looking up from the wire he was twisting, 'well, the drake maybe, if he had a bump on his nose.'

'You see, you know them all,' she shook her head. 'I wish I did.'

'Well, not all,' he said modestly, 'but a fair number.'

'That eider duck you showed me,' Jane went on, 'I always thought eiderdown was a sort of trade name, like a hoover. But those ducks, they are such a dark, dreary colour, not at all like the inside of a duvet.'

'If you would see the nest of an eider duck in May,' said the old man, with his rare smile, 'all lined with the soft feathers from her breast, and if you were to lay your hand in it, you would think you had found the nest for an angel.'

Jane's delighted laugh at his analogy surprised and pleased him, and he was silent while he thought about it. Never in his memory had anyone made him feel his knowledge was of value or his words were worth attention. This strange creature who had invaded his life actually seemed to find him interesting and to enjoy listening to him. It was an extraordinary new sensation and not an unpleasant one.

She was beginning to know his moods, and, as the days went by, to recognise the times when her silence would draw more from him than her questions. Sometimes an ill-considered word from her would stop him short in the middle of a description or an explanation, and then it was as if he could not, rather than would not, continue. He reminded her of an engine that had lain long in rusty disuse and whose various parts were learning, erratically, to turn again. There was an art in keeping him going for longer and longer periods without a hitch, and she was getting better at avoiding the verbal jerks that would bring him to a standstill, when his eyes became evasive and his words monosyllabic. She had learnt that he would not discuss his neighbours and if she talked about herself he became embarrassed.

He was never intentionally funny and was unaware of how entertaining she found his expressions or that she carefully committed to memory his more unusual turns of phrase. She doubted if she could reproduce the precision with which he selected his words, choosing them as if they were from a box of colours, and then using those colours in unexpected ways and places. She wondered if he translated his thoughts from the Gaelic, and whether the long pauses and slow delivery were to give him time to perfect the grammar of each sentence. He never spoke carelessly.

For John Donald, the threat the girl had seemed to represent was slowly receding and the summer was falling back into its normal tranquil pattern. He would certainly not have considered that he enjoyed the company of 'the lassie' – he had forgotten her name, even supposing he had taken it in during the confused moments of their first meeting – but her daily visits no longer caused him any discomfort; rather the opposite, in fact, and it even crossed his mind, disloyally, that his grandfather could, just possibly, as far as women were concerned, be mistaken.

One day when Jane failed to turn up he felt mildly put out; he had been planning to bring in and pack a consignment of lobsters, and she had expressed an interest in seeing them prepared for travel.

He made no comment, however, when she appeared the following day, and he was embarrassed that she found it necessary to explain how she had not come because she wanted to get some work finished, and some letters for the mail-boat. He was slightly disturbed, too, by her mention of work. It made him feel unsure again, this new light on her, as he had thought of her as on holiday. He would not have dreamt of enquiring the nature of her work.

Jane was pleased John Donald had delayed packing the lobsters, and even more pleased when he held the boat against the rock, showing she was expected to join him for the short trip to the lobster keep floating a hundred yards offshore. It was the first time she had set foot in his boat; recognising that his fishing expeditions were his most private enjoyment she had not yet ventured to suggest accompanying him.

Back on land, she examined the shiny blue-black creatures, admiring the dappling on the shells where the blue faded to a creamy colour on the sides of the overlapping armour plating. She teased one with a blade of grass, making its long antennae twitch.

'I suppose I always thought they were red, like in a restaurant,' she said. 'Yet I vaguely knew they only turn red when they are cooked. They are really beautiful like this.'

'I have never seen a lobster cooked,' said John Donald.

She had wild thoughts of raw lobster on a plate, with a tin mug of tea beside it, and then said carefully:

'You don't eat lobster, then?'

'And why would I be wanting to eat lobster?'

'It's very good.'

'Well, it must be,' he replied, 'the price they will pay.'

Together they packed the lobsters in wooden fish boxes John Donald had gleaned from the beaches after the winter storms. Each was neatly labelled requesting its return to J. D. MacQueen, Dunbeag, Torisay. They tucked the gleaming tails under and stretched the claws forward as they fitted the creatures closely together, nose to tail, covering each living layer and filling the gaps with sun-dried bladderwrack gathered from the shore.

'Wouldn't wet seaweed make better packing for them?' said Jane.

'They will travel a long way as long as they are dry,' said John Donald, 'and come to no harm at all.'

'It must be horrible for them, all the same.'

'Those that will be eating them will not be thinking of that.'

'How will you get them to the mail-boat?' she asked, when the lid had been nailed on the second box.

'There is a man, Willie Lamont, will lift them in his van from the road-end in the morning. I will take them up early while it is still cool.'

'Can I come over and help you carry them?'

'At five o'clock?' he smiled. 'The boat is early coming.'

'I'd like to.'

'If you have a mind to,' he said, 'there is nothing to stop you.'

She arrived at a run as dawn was turning into day, her face bright with excitement.

He was standing by the shed.

'John Donald,' she panted, 'I saw an otter, the most beautiful otter, just standing there by the burn, as close as you are, looking at me! I've never seen anything so … so amazing!'

'Have you never seen an otter? Maybe you have never been up in the light of the morning before? This time belongs to the beasts, and they have no fear for you then.'

'No, really, it had no fear.' She was still aglow with her experience. 'And when it had finished looking at me it just turned and slithered into the water.'

'Yes,' he said. 'They live in the burn. Sometimes, when it is quiet, you will see them come down into the bay. The sea is their country too.'

They each took an end of the first lobster box, and after two trips up the track they sat side by side on the bench in front of the house, sipping tea out of chipped enamel mugs. The tide was ebbing, and the sloping sunlight cast long shadows from the rocks out across the glistening sand. The pale gold sea was as still as glass, and a purple haze masked the hills on the distant mainland.

'It's going to be a fantastic day,' said Jane.

'Aye, it will.'

'What will you be doing?'

'After the sheep? Well,' he said thoughtfully, 'it would be a day for a flounder line.'

'What's a flounder line?'

'If you stay you will be able to see.'

'All right.'

And so it happened; the invitation he had not been going to give, the invitation she had not dared ask for, was given and accepted without a ripple of disturbance. Jane had the feeling she was striking gold.

By the time the chores around the croft were finished, the tide was well out. They walked down the exposed beach, splashing through puddles that mirrored the colour of the clear sky, to where lugworm coils were beginning to appear at the water's edge. John Donald Sōa began to dig, turning over forkfuls of dark wet sand with a regular motion.

'You pick the worms,' he said.

'Where?' said Jane.

'You have to be quick,' he said, pointing to where a little cliff of exposed sand broke away into the seeping water and she saw a shiny dark brown shape sliding out of sight. She swooped and drew it out.

'Yuck,' she said, grimacing at the limp form hanging over her finger, not slimy but fleshy and unattractive.

'Drop it in the pail.' He was digging again. 'There is another, look.'

After half an hour the bucket was half full, and they were sitting on the bench. John Donald had produced a coiled line from the lean-to, a thick line, dark brown and stiff with salt and age. There were hooks on droppers attached every yard or so along its length. A worm was to be impaled on every hook, a process Jane found repulsive, then bearable, and finally boring. She reflected as she worked on the patience of the fisherman '… his time is set by the tide, his only imperative its rise and fall…' and rather liked the ring of it.

'One hundred,' said John Donald, as he lifted the coiled and fully baited line.

'Bring that fish box,' he said to her over his shoulder, 'and waste no time. The tide is nearly out.'

He was treating her with a new familiarity.

There was not a breath of wind. The little boat chugged over the limpid water, causing the only ripples on the still surface. It was so clear near the shore that, looking over the side, Jane could easily make out the marks on the sand of the green seabed and patches of waving weed growing on underwater rocks.

After about ten minutes, crossing deeper, darker water, John Donald slowed the engine and peered over the side.

'There is a sandbank here, running up this way towards the point there. We will set the line from here and maybe we will not be doing it for nothing.'

A round plastic float was attached to the end of the line, and some yards along from it a lead weight. As the boat moved slowly along Jane fed the hooks over the side until she came to the weight and float at the other end. At a nod from John Donald she dropped them into the water.

'How long do you leave it?' she said.

'Until the tide is well turned,' he replied. 'More than an hour.'

This will be a good time to get him talking, she thought, while he is relaxed and enjoying himself. But John Donald had no thought of relaxing.

'We will lift the creels,' he said, and revving up the engine, swung the boat round and set off north-eastwards towards a distant headland. They passed a low line of rocks where seals, their coats dry and silvery, basked in the warmth of the sun. They turned their heads and watched the passing boat with huge dark eyes.

'They are so tame,' said Jane. 'Would we be able to get closer to them? I would love to get a photograph.'

It came out of her pocket, the object John Donald had seen at first with such aversion. But she was careful never to turn it towards him when he was looking.

He turned the boat towards the rocks and hushed the engine, but before they were two boat-lengths away all the seals had humped and slithered their way into the sea, their big cocoon-like bodies far more agile than they had first appeared. Sleek dark seal heads popped out of the water all round the boat, staring, much bolder in their own element.

'They look like dogs now,' whispered Jane, 'black Labradors.'

'If you were in there yourself they would let you close to them,' said John Donald. 'They have no fear for you under the water.'

'I'd love to try,' she said. 'Have you ever swum with seals?'

'I cannot swim,' he replied.

Jane was only a little surprised. She had noticed during the best weather that though she had seen some obvious trippers splashing in the surf, none of the islanders ever seemed to take to the water except in boats. The sea is their farm, she thought, not their playground. That was how she would put it.

As they passed round the headland a line of yellow floats came in into sight. John Donald showed her how to haul in and coil the slimy ropes and finally to heave the heavy creels into the boat. The first two were empty, but the third came over the side with flashes of blue within its netting. John Donald quickly untied the entrance and pulled two big lobsters out, holding them behind the shoulders, their claws flailing impotently. Jane exclaimed in excitement, and John Donald smiled, seeing her draw her feet up on the seat as they scrabbled about in the bottom of the boat. Deftly he tied their claws with twine, gripping their bodies between his knees and keeping an eye on the nearby rocks as he did. But the sea was as calm as ever, and the boat hardly moved.

For two hours they moved along the coast, lifting creels, and then returned to the flounder line. On every fourth or fifth hook they found a fish – 'flatties', John Donald called them. Occasionally a whiting or small cod appeared, till soon they had a box full of flapping, sliding shapes. Jane learned to take them off the hooks without impaling herself, and to tell the varieties by their fins and markings.

'In the Gaelic a cod fish and an old man have the same name,' said John Donald. 'It is because they each have a beard under their chin.'

She watched as with a skilful knife and practiced fingers he gutted the fish, a cloud of herring gulls hovering above the boat and swooping with raucous cries on each scrap of offal as he threw it into the sea. Jane was fascinated by their aerial agility and repelled by their hard yellow eyes.

'They look so cruel,' she said.

'It is the black-backs that are the cruel ones,' said John Donald. 'They will take a new-born lamb at its mother's side and peck out its eyes.'

'How horrible.'

He smiled.

'There is no creature made by God that is not cruel to some other creature. We cannot help it. It is in our nature.'

The sun was getting low by the time they rounded the little grass-topped rock of Sōa, once again isolated at the mouth of the bay. The land lay placid and golden and only the hills were dark against the brilliant evening sky. Long vaporous trails of cloud streamed across the heavens, each turning a glowing face towards the radiance in the west, and with their lighted flanks even the rocks seemed to have turned to watch the glory of the sunset. The boat, sliding silently into the bay, the engine cut, made the only movement in the unrippled stillness of the water.

It seemed to Jane that she had never consciously been surrounded by so much beauty and peace. She felt a longing to retain it, somehow to express it in words. Timeless, she tried, untouched by the real world, breathless tranquillity – trite clichés only downgraded what she was experiencing and did not convey at all the glow of happy unreality washing round her. Her cheeks glowed, too, from their long exposure to the sun. She had not come equipped for this. She wondered if they sold after-sun lotion in the store and doubted it.

The dogs ran down the sand towards them, barking and circling in their joy.

'What will you do with all that fish,' she asked, as they unloaded the boat.

'Maybe I will eat some,' he said. 'And bait, bait for the creels. Some days there will be no fish, but the creels have to be baited. I will salt it all and put it in the bait barrel after you have gone.'

She took her cue, and collected her coat from the bows, preparing for the walk back to the road.

'Would you mind if I took one or two flounders? I am sure they would cook them for me at the hotel.'

John Donald looked aside, then straightened his cap unnecessarily upon his head.

'It is better not,' he said. 'They would ask where you had been.'

She opened her mouth and shut it again.

Then, 'Good night,' she said, 'and thank you. It's been a wonderful day.'

'You get home before it is dark,' said John Donald, without looking at her.

She left him, and as always when he was alone, he felt he was accompanied. But something in his mood gave him a determination not to allow that all-pervading grandfatherly presence to creep into his consciousness with its disapproval. Mentally he shouldered his way past it, and walked up towards his house, feeling as daringly positive as he had on the day he left school.

The fine weather held, and Jane's daily visits to the croft became packed with experience such as she had never known in her life. It was as if a floodgate had opened within John Donald; all the knowledge he had gathered during his solitary life was pouring out, not often in expression of thought or opinion but more in showing, telling, demonstrating everything he knew about the sea and the land he worked, and about the birds and beasts that inhabited them both.

He taught Jane the names of the fish they caught in English, and, when his English failed him, in the soft Gaelic words which seemed to suit them better. He showed her how to attract to her line the big golden lythe which haunted the underwater groves of waving tangle weed, and how to deal with the great eels which sometimes came up in the creels, writhing, twisting lengths of muscle a yard or more long and as thick as a man's arm. He taught her to steer the boat, and to use the small engine to hold them off the rocks as they lifted the creels in rough water. She came to handle lobsters with a nonchalance she could not have imagined at the start of the summer, and to outwit the stubborn brown crabs which could be as hard as limpets to prise from the bottom of a creel.

On balmy, windless days they would go far out to sea and anchor over the cod bank, where sand rose to within thirty feet of the surface. Their weighted lines hung vertically below them and the boat rocked gently in the barely noticeable swell. In the quiet periods when the fish were not taking their bait John Donald would talk of his childhood and of his grandfather.

His love for the old man who had been his only real friend was evident in all he said, but Jane noted signs of respect that could equate with fear. No word of criticism of the patriarch ever passed his lips, and she felt rather than heard him lower his voice when he spoke of him. At some stage of the reminiscence he would always repeat the mantra, 'He was a good man. He taught me all I know.'

Jane came to know some of the signs that would indicate to John Donald whether or not it was safe to take his small craft out in the notoriously dangerous Hebridean waters. White caps on waves beyond a certain rock a quarter of a mile out to sea; a southeasterly wind; a startling clarity in the hills on the mainland; a distant creeping fog – all these meant a likelihood that he would say, 'It is not a day for the boat.' He also listened without fail to the shipping forecast on the ancient Pye radio which he referred to as the wireless and which was, as far as she knew, never turned on for any other purpose. However innocent a day might look to Jane's eyes, nothing would persuade him to take his boat out if the forecast or his instincts said no, and she had seen his caution justified more than once when a grey fog swept in and within seconds obscured even the rocks at the point of the bay, or a Force 9 gale grew within hours from a mild early morning breeze. Equally, no degree of perfection in the weather would persuade him to lift a creel or catch fish on a Sunday. He was shocked when Jane first expressed her surprise at this, and shaking his head gently explained to her:

'It would not do at all to be doing such things on the Sabbath. There are six days for these.'

When the sea was forbidden, once his work was done they would go along the shore. He showed her where to find the dark red fringes of carragheen weed below the lowest tide-mark.

'My grandfather never had the rheumatics in all his days, and that was from eating the carragheen.'

He named for Jane the flowers growing in the close packed machair turf, the eyebright, the pale Hebridean orchid, the scarlet pimpernel, the nodding head of the butterwort, the tiny blue gentian and countless others making up the multi-coloured carpet on which his sheep found their grazing.

She learned to distinguish the calls of the oystercatcher and the whaup and stood gazing up in amazement at the sound and sight of a snipe 'drumming' as it patrolled its territory with staggering climbs and falls. John Donald took her to a rocky promontory where a flock of greylag geese had spent the night on a grassy mound, leaving their droppings scattered over half an acre of grass which they had mown like a lawn.

He showed her the decaying body of a young whale which had stranded itself on a shingly strand the previous spring and laughed at her face when she accidentally placed herself downwind of the corpse. He pointed out a family of porpoises enjoying themselves a few hundred yards offshore, rolling over and over like a procession of black rubber tyres.

They watched gannets soaring high above a shoal of fish and then, folding their wings like paper darts, tipped by their long yellow beaks, plunging vertically into the waves to rise again seconds later with their prey already sliding down their bulging throats.

'There is so much,' she said. 'I never realised there was so much.'

'It would take more than your life to see all there is on this island,' he replied.

Sometimes, in the evening, when the beach and the rocks were dark but the dying sun still drew a luminous glow from the sea, they would sit out on the bench with mugs of coffee and drams of whisky. Then John Donald would repeat old stories and island legends his grandfather had been told as a boy. When the sun finally set and the night chill seeped up from the sea they went indoors and in the flickering light of burning driftwood in the hearth the tales of ghostly pipers who were heard before some tragic event and of strange dark cavorting creatures which would lure a man to his death in the waves grew eerily real.

One night, as she rose to leave, it suddenly occurred to John Donald that he might have made the lassie nervous.

'I'll walk up the path with you,' he said, 'and see you on your way.'

'Thanks, John Donald,' she said gratefully, 'just in case I meet a kelpie!'

There was a ring of pale haze round the full moon which lit the narrow track, and Jane tried to remember what this might mean in terms of the weather.

'There will be a change,' said John Donald. 'The wind is backing to the south.'

He stopped on a rise a little short of the road.

'I will watch you to your car.'

Jane started the engine and switched on the headlights. As she stared down the narrow tarmac road she felt as usual that she was passing into a different world, but tonight she did it with a reluctant resentment. She preferred the world she had just left behind down by the bay. Lately she had come to see the relationship she had developed with John Donald as something very rare and delicate, and she was suddenly worried that this precious thing she had created and nurtured was at risk. She never normally found it hard to separate her private enjoyment from her work, even when they apparently overlapped. But now, for the first time, and perhaps because the second glass of whisky had undermined her professionalism, she felt disturbed. She found herself facing the fact that she was about to commit an act of unspeakable betrayal.

'For God's sake,' she said aloud, 'you're drunk.'

And a little way down the road she told herself not to think now, but to think in the morning. She must think about it all seriously in the morning.

It was as John Donald kicked the embers of his dying fire together that he noticed the black notebook lying on the floor by the chair in which Jane has been sitting. He stood looking down at it for a long moment, and then he turned and climbed the narrow stair to the loft, leaving it lying where it was.

The wind began to rise in the night, and in the first light of dawn John Donald rose to make sure his boat was riding safely on its mooring. There was a murky yellowness in the dark clouds on the horizon. He thought of the herring trawlers which had anchored for a night off the island three days earlier, and wondered where they were now. His boat was securely tied, as always, but nevertheless he put an extra hitch in the rope.

Jane appeared in the early afternoon, her camera slung round her neck as usual, fighting against the wind that filled her anorak and doubled her bulk. She found John Donald attaching extra stones to the ropes which held down the small haystacks behind the steadings.

'What a day!' she called, turning her back to the bay and leaning against the buffeting blast. 'I have been down to the other end of the island all morning, on the rocks beyond Cean Bodha, trying to get some good shots of the waves. They never look so good through the viewfinder, unless you get almost under them, and then you get the lens wet. I thought I'd go to the point and try there. I could see the spray rising as I came down the track.'

'Aye,' said John Donald, without looking at her or pausing in his work.

'What's the forecast like?'

'Very poor. Rising Force 9, so they say.'

'I'd like to see that. John Donald, did I leave a notebook behind last night?'

'You did. You will find it on the dresser.'

She stood for a moment silently beside him and finally he stood up to face her. He was about to speak, but she had turned and was walking towards the croft house.

The notebook was lying where he had said. Jane picked it up and held it in her hand as if weighing it, gazing out of the window, and seeing nothing. How much, she wondered, had he read? Had he read any of it? It would not be in his character, as she knew it, to pry into something which belonged to someone else. He had never asked her a single question about herself. She pushed the book well down into her anorak pocket. She thought, on the whole, he would not have looked at it. In any case, it didn't matter now. She had made up her mind since the day before that she would never use those notes.

She felt he was watching her as she climbed the rocks towards the point and she turned on the highest one, precarious in the wind, to wave at him. He picked up his tools and walked into the steading.

Jane had not been out of sight for more than five minutes when a small boy came running down the track, leaping the heather tussocks. The dogs ran barking to greet him. As he drew nearer John Donald recognised him as the son of the postmaster, younger brother of the girl in the post office.

'Hello Lachy,' he said.

'Hello, John Donald,' said the lad, panting and running grubby fingers through his windblown hair, 'Is the lady, that Miss Parker here?'

John Donald stared at him.

'What?' he said. Then he knew.

'The lady with Alec MacBride's car. It's up near the Brodach road-end.'

'There's … there's a lady gone down the beach,' said John Donald.

'I've a message for her from my Dad. Will you give it to her?'

'What message?'

'Ach, it's this man,' said the boy, shrugging. 'He's been on the telephone all day to speak to her. It's about deadlines, and copy or something, that kinna thing, and she's to telephone him at his office and she's to get the message right away my Dad says. Here, it's on this.'

He thrust a much-folded scrap of paper at John Donald and wiped his nose with the back of his hand.

'OK, John Donald, you'll give it her? OK? Cheerio, John Donald. Can I have this wee bit rope? OK?'

He was off up the track while John Donald was still absorbing the meaning of the gabbled words.

When Jane returned an hour later John Donald was sitting on the bench where the porch gave some shelter from the wind. She was surprised. He seldom sat down before the evening unless it was to work from that position. But his hands were clasped together between his knees.

She dropped down beside him and brushed the wind-matted hair from her eyes.

'It's wild, really wild, out there,' she said. 'Just marvellous. No wonder the rocks end up in weird shapes with waves like that beating on them year after year. And the clouds, I have never seen them moving like that. They are just galloping, roaring across the sky, look!'

'There was a message for you,' said John Donald, pulling the note from his pocket.

She unfolded and read it.

'Oh, blast,' she said. 'I'll have to go. It's from my agent. I've got to ring him before four, and it must be nearly that now. Right, then, see you tomorrow, weather permitting!'

She turned to smile at him as she rose and was taken aback by the expression on his face as he looked up at her.

Oh, sh ... sugar, she thought, I haven't got time to explain.

'I'll be over tomorrow, honestly, John Donald. I just have to run now.'

She was moving away but turned her head once more to find his gaze still on her. Then she was round the corner of the house and running up the track. After a while she slowed to a walk, panting, and turned again for a moment, the wind whipping her hair across her face, to look at the back of the croft house as it sat in its hollow at the edge of the bay. Was he still sitting there, still wearing that expression? Her habit of putting things into facile phrases came over her. Dumb bewilderment, was it? Confused questioning? Wordless disbelief? She was being over-dramatic, of course. He was just disappointed by her brief visit and surprised at her hurry. He was not one for impetuous behaviour.

It was as she was driving fast down the road to Torisay, her thoughts on the difficult conversation ahead, that the words 'blind despair' flashed across her mind, and for a second she thought she knew what she had seen. No, surely not. That really was exaggeration. Anyway, it was too late to turn back now. She would go early and put it all right in the morning, whatever it was.

Down by the bay John Donald still sat on his bench. Since early in the day his mind had been whirling with confused thoughts, and now it was almost numb with pain. He would never have laid a hand on that notebook, had not one of the dogs lifted it from where it lay on the floor and carried it into a corner with the apparent intention of chewing it. John Donald rescued it and put it on the table where it lay at the edge of his vision and dominated his thoughts as he ate his simple breakfast.

Eventually, and suddenly, thrusting aside the sense of shame that had been holding him back, giving way to the overwhelming curiosity which had been devouring him, he stretched out a hand and drew it towards him. Even so it was minutes before he opened it.

He flicked over the pages, glancing only fleetingly at the unrelated sentences, as though to convince himself that he was not really reading it. Then, as his eyes grew used to the clear, rather childish writing, the sense of the words became real in his mind. He read each page through to the end. His mug of tea grew cold on the table beside him.

With rising dismay he realised the description he read must be of himself – 'skin corrugated by wind and weather' – 'generations of sea-faring experience lie behind the sea-blue eyes' – 'one sister, died, how old?' – 'tending his boat as another man might care for a favourite horse' – 'a lamb, like a child's toy in the gnarled brown hands'…

He recognised his own expressions, his own ideas that he had put into words, just for her – 'the sun will stroke the island into bloom' – 'a south wind you can do nothing with' – 'there is no love in the sea, only a great desire' – (of a row of cormorants on a rock) 'The Kirk Session, disapproving…'

Worst of all, he read notes on his grandfather, and he could only recognise the details as coming from himself – 'Long beard, stroked it when he was at peace' – 'No harder on others than he was on himself' – 'born 1846?' – 'no love for the elders of the Kirk' – 'Never mentions grandmother – why? Were they married?' – 'JD clearly frightened of him' – 'Fierce eyes, but a Good Man'…

And there was more, much more.

John Donald's chin dropped to his chest, and his eyes closed. He was in shock. The flush of blood that had at first suffused his face seemed to have travelled to his gut, and he felt cold and sick. It was as if he had been stripped naked in front of a jeering crowd.

He was aware of his grandfather's presence standing behind him, reading over his shoulder, and he felt the weight of its cold disdain. The depth of the shame he felt was increased by the knowledge that he had gone against all that he had ever believed. He had allowed his life to be entered by a stranger, a female stranger; he had not 'kept himself to himself' in any sense. He had opened his very soul.

It was typical of the old crofter's generosity of character that he felt no resentment towards Jane – the fault, as he saw it, was entirely in himself: he deserved this punishment after his foolishness, and that presence at his shoulder would give him neither sympathy nor relief in his humiliation.

What now? What would she do with all she had taken from him? Should he destroy the book? He knew this was no solution. No, he would have to talk with her, and reason with her. What had been in those letters she wrote and sent on the mail-boat? Was it already too late? His head ached with the intensity of his mortification at the idea of his words existing somewhere out of his control. But, of course, writing them down did not necessarily mean she would show them to anyone else, did it? Surely not. She was a good lassie; he had felt she was good, he had trusted her, and felt safe with her. She would surely not betray him. He would speak with her, pluck up his courage when she came later in the day. She would listen.

He had set about his tasks that morning like an automaton, his mind gnawing at his problem, practising the words he would use, his eyes ever on the rise behind the house over which she must appear.

But when at last she came, she was in a hurry, she wanted to go up to the point of the bay with her camera. He nearly spoke when she asked for her notebook, but while he was looking for the words she went into the house, and instead of coming back she went away up the rocks. He would speak when she came back, he thought. But then the boy had come with the note. Reading it, he realised it had all gone too far. Deadline … copy … typescript … Not just a writer, she was, but a journalist. John Donald did not take a newspaper, but he had often read the pages of the tabloid paper wrapping his groceries. He knew about journalists.

He thought briefly of concealing the note from her, but he was morally incapable of it. Perhaps as she read it he would be able to speak. But she was so quick. She was up, keen to be away.

For a moment, and for the first time, he felt a sense of hurt, of betrayal, but only for a moment. She was only doing her job. It was he, John Donald, who had betrayed, and it was that shadowy presence, he and he only, who was entitled to feel that faith had been broken.

She had smiled, and she had seemed to be leering at him, and it was like a foretaste of the laughter which would sweep the island when they heard, when they read. They would laugh at the photographs, they would laugh in the bar, and the whole world would hear the mocking laughter.

And his grandfather would hear the laughter, and the degradation would engulf them both.

Dusk came early, hastened by the heavy clouds, and it was nearly dark when John Donald finally got to his feet. He fed his dogs and shut them in the house before walking to the shore. The tide was in and the massive waves sweeping into the bay had the boat straining and bucketing on its mooring. With difficulty he untied the wet rope from the ring on the rock.

The wind was still strong the following morning, carrying away the wild flurries of spray which were flung up as the waves burst upon the rocks. But the slanting, stinging rain had died away, and a patch of brilliant blue sky was spreading along the horizon to the south. The gale that had flailed the island throughout the night was still blowing, but with diminished fervour.

Jane walked fast down the familiar path, splashing through puddles of peaty brown water. The dogs usually ran to greet her, barking, as she came over the rise, but today there was no sign of them. Perhaps John Donald was still out at the sheep – it could take longer to check them after a wild night.

As she rounded the corner of the house she was surprised to hear the dogs barking inside. Indoors? In the daytime? This was unheard of. Could John Donald be ill? She tried the door. It was on the latch, and as she pushed it inwards the collies rushed through the gap and greeted her with hysterical barks and leaps, whining and licking her face and hands. They had never reacted to her like this before.

She pushed them down and went into the house. The fire was out and she felt the place was empty, but she called John Donald's name all the same.

She went outside again and looked for the first time down to where the dogs were sniffing about by the water's edge. The wind carried their anxious whines back to her.

She saw then that the boat was not on its mooring. She gasped. John Donald would never take his boat out in weather like this, never risk his boat or his life in those vicious waves! In fact, it would not be just taking a risk, it would be simple suicide. The word hit her like a kick in the stomach. The deep unease that had been nagging at her since she had left the croft the previous day surged up in her as a wave of realisation and horror.

'Oh, Jesus, oh my God, John Donald…'

She broke into a stumbling run towards the shore, sobbing into the wind, 'I must get up there … he'll see me … I must stop him, o-oh stop him.'

The dogs ran back gratefully towards her, barking excitedly as she stumbled into the sea, her boots filling with water as she fell forward into a breaking wave. Momentarily shocked by the cold, she staggered to her feet and began to wade towards where the rocks of the point were still cut off by the tide. The water dragged on her legs, holding her back; it was like trying to run in a dream.

'John Donald, for goodness sake, I won't do it … I told them

I wouldn't do it ... I told them I wouldn't go on, it's all over, I won't do it ... John Donald!'

Her cries were blown back into her face.

The rocks were covered in wet weed, and her heavy boots could get little grip on their slippery sides as she dragged herself out of the water. She climbed higher, her fingernails breaking on the barnacles and the blood ran from her grazed knees. The point of the rocks had never seemed so far away, and she could hardly tell if she was going in the right direction, for her eyes were blinded by tears and the wind blew her hair across her face. She stumbled forward, slipping and falling into treacherous crevices, moaning all the time:

'I didn't do it, John Donald, I didn't do it...'

She stood at last on the highest point of the promontory and looked out on the wide expanse of tossing, grey, featureless sea. The wind whipped off the white crests of the waves in long trails of spume, but nothing else moved on the water except the cold-eyed herring gulls, wheeling ceaselessly over its surface.

Her legs felt weak, and she sank on her knees in exhaustion and despair. Then she threw back her head and screamed into the sky:

'Oh my God, John Donald, could you be so bloody stupid?'

John Donald Sōa's boat was never found, but his body was washed up forty-eight hours later a mile down the coast. The inquest, which Jane returned to the island to attend, was short and to the point, as was its finding – 'death by misadventure'. There were mutterings at the back of the school hall to the effect that 'while balance of mind disturbed' would have made more sense.

'He had to be out of his mind to take his boat out in a south-easterly gale...'

The funeral service was held two days later in the small stone church overlooking the harbour, and was well attended, though Jane was not aware of any tears shed other than her own. She would have liked to follow the coffin bearers to the grave in the cemetery at the back of the village but was informed that this was a 'men only' affair. She stood watching their retreating backs as they processed up the narrow track, their dark suits and bowler hats contrasting starkly with the sunlit green of the machair and its late summer flowers.

She was warmly invited to the post-funeral feast, however, and was taken aback by the jollity of the occasion, when whisky, neat, with water or with lemonade flowed freely till quite late in the evening. She wondered how many of the people there actually knew John Donald. And she thought how glad John Donald would have been not to be present.

She stood at the rail in the stern of the boat the next morning, looking back at the island as it became a line of rocks sinking lower and lower into the sea. She would never come back, she knew, and she would never write the island profile she had planned. But some day, when she could face it, she would try to write about John Donald. She would not use his name, because he would not like that. Some other name, she would give him.

She would begin, 'John Archie MacLeod was an essentially private man.'

MAIRI

1960s

'That Archie, he has a heart of gold and a throat like an open drain,' said Neil the Pump.

His wife, May, walked from where she had been standing at her kitchen door across the small yard to where he stood.

Together they watched the grey mini-van as it progressed slowly through the dusk up the narrow road out of Torisay village in a succession of serpentine curves which took it to the edge of the grass on either side of the road alternately.

'It's just as well,' she said, 'there's no ditches between here and Brodach. And it's just as well Cameron's away down to Baide-anach or he'd be after him.'

Neil turned to examine the dent inflicted on his petrol pump as Archie had reversed in the eighth and final manoeuvre of what had been intended as a three-point turn. The cover of the pump had not been what you might call pristine for some while, since it had stood by the repair shed for nearly seven years, dispensing petrol to all the motor-mobile members of the community.

Indeed the star symbols were hardly discernible now, which did not matter because he only sold 2-star petrol anyway. He had got the big pump as an economy since, as May would explain cynically, he had had 'plans for expansion'. Expansion had not been necessary however, because 2-star was what everybody wanted for their outboard motors, and nobody had ever asked for any petrol for their cars other than the pump provided. They were grateful that Neil was willing to serve them at virtually any time of day or night, and Archie, turning up as he had just done when the bar at the hotel closed, had been sure that his van would get a full tank.

'I'll get the cover off easy enough and knock it out with a hammer,' said Neil, 'and it will be as good as new.'

'Here he's back again,' said May.

The mini-van, still in second gear, came slowly back down the Brodach road and turning in pulled up beside them. The engine stalled. After some fumbling Archie found the handle and wound the window creakily down into the moss-rimmed depths of the door.

'I was just wondering,' he said, 'whether by any chance I would have left my wee dog with you, by any chance?'

'She's sitting right behind you in the van,' said Neil the Pump, nodding at the narrow black head and intelligent brown eyes that watched him from behind Archie's back.

'Is that so?' said Archie, switching on his interior light and peering, stiff-necked, first over one shoulder, then the other. 'There she is right enough. Well, I wouldn't want to be losing her at all. I'll be away home then. Thank you very much.'

'Put your side-lights on, Archie,' said Neil.

'I will. I will do that.'

In a series of diminishing bounds the van set off again in the Balinbeag direction.

'He's away the wrong way,' said May unnecessarily.

They stood waiting for the van's inevitable return before retiring to their house for the night.

'It's himself would be lost without that dog, I'm sure she does Archie's thinking for him when he's in that state. It's just a shame she can't drive.'

'She's a grand wee dog for the sheep, too,' said her husband. 'She can drive them, right enough. It's never a word he has to say to her when she's working. She'll be well up in years now though.'

The van passed again, on its original route, and by the interior light they could see Archie leaning well forward and holding the steering wheel tightly under his chin with both hands. He released one of them for a quick wave and continued his erratic course homewards. A long streamer of bracken trailed from his rear bumper.

Mairi MacPhail was making oatcakes. She opened the door of her electric stove and peered anxiously into its interior.

Until fairly recently, her Friday night oatcake-making had been a time of pure relaxation and pleasure. She had used the old iron girdle that had belonged to her mother and before that to her grandmother. She had heated it on top of the well-blacked range in the deep alcove at one end of her kitchen. Sipping a cup of tea that was an important part of the ritual, she would watch the flat grey triangles gradually change colour before she lifted them with her spatula and set them to dry in front of the open door of the fire, just as she had seen her mother do when she was young.

The range squatted benignly in the alcove, a living presence in the low-ceilinged kitchen, the warm heart of the small croft house, and she would never be without it. It kept the room at a cosy temperature in summer and winter and kept at a perpetual simmer the black tin kettle that sat upon it so that it was always ready at a moment's notice to provide the comfort of a cup of tea.

But she had recently persuaded Archie that she would not be content, or leave him alone, until she also had a modern electric cooker.

Archie, a kindly man who had no objection to his wife updating her image, had pored with her over a pile of brochures supplied by the West of Scotland Hydro-Electric Board. They had discussed together and at length the merits of different oven sizes. Mairi, accepting cheerfully that the need to cook a twenty-pound turkey would probably not arise, but feeling that there was something demeaning in picking the smallest turkey-size oven, insisted on the fourteen-pound model.

Archie knew that Mairi was unlikely suddenly to emulate Elisabeth, wife of Zacharia, and start a family so late in life; thus nothing larger than a chicken, scrawny and tough from many years of egg-production, was ever likely to cross their oven threshold; but he acquiesced cheerfully in her choice.

She had been a good wife to him. He had never regretted the impulse that had overtaken him late one night thirty years earlier when, sitting beside her at a post-sheep-sale ceilidh at the church hall, he had nudged her elbow and said:

'Well then, Mairi, you and me, how about it? Are you willing?'

Mairi had blushed. 'Och you, Archie MacPhail…'

Then she had given him a charming sideways glance and said: 'Well, why not?'

Six months later she had become Mrs Archibald MacPhail and joined him in the family croft house where she had taken up the tasks recently relinquished by Archie's deceased mother. The old range once again billowed with clouds of smoke in the early morning, with steam from the clothes boiler at midday, and with warm reassuring smells of bubbling broth or porridge in the evening. There was no 'convenience food' to be seen in their house and Mairi would have been shamed by the thought of taking a potato scone from a packet.

Archie was content. Probably no words of love passed between him and Mairi after the early days but they were not needed by either of them. There were no words of anger either and they often had a good laugh together. There had been no children, but then you can't have everything, and a good dog is as useful as a handy lad on a croft; there was no doubt his old Meg was the best worker, not to say the best friend, that Archie had ever known.

No, he had no regrets but rather a great deal to be thankful for in his marriage. And if Mairi wanted his thanks in the form of an electric stove Mairi was welcome to it.

So it was ordered and arrived on the ferry some weeks later. It was brought from the pier by Willie Lamont in the back of his big van. Willie helped Mairi to remove vast quantities of cardboard and polystyrene to reveal the awesome control panel of the new cooker, and left, saying:

'Well, you'll be needing a licence to drive that one, Mairi, so you will.'

Mairi had been privately appalled by the number of dials and knobs confronting her but by sheer determination and endless perusal of the instruction book she had mastered the complexities of the machine. By now, in theory at least, she could have gone away for a week and returned to find a three-course meal ready to serve to a party of eight. In practice, however, it had simply removed the confidence she normally felt in her cooking. With the range she just knew instinctively when the heat was right and how to adjust it by opening the oven door or by stoking up the fire. But these dials and degrees and buzzers simply led to burnt food and things that had never even started to cook by the time they were needed.

Now she found herself unable to relax over her tea, and she had constantly to peer through the glass to see that her oatcakes were not turning black. She was sorely tempted to take down the familiar girdle from where it hung above the range, but pride prevented it.

It was into the glowing heart of the range, however, that she gazed as she thought about her other worry that Friday night.

By long-standing arrangement Mairi's baking night was Archie's evening out. For eighteen years he had spent every Friday evening in Torisay, in the bar of the only hotel on the island. It was an occasion to meet and converse with the other menfolk, since it was not the custom for women to go there, unless they were trippers. They talked, Mairi supposed, about lamb prices, prospects for the hay and barley harvest and, she thought vaguely, world affairs. There was a manliness about all this. It suited the image she treasured of 'my Archie' that he should have this weekly indulgence. He was a good and, she believed, faithful husband, unlike some she could name, and a man deserved a while to himself every now and then.

She did not resent at all the fact that he always came home considerably the worse for the whisky that he had consumed and often several hours after closing time. The effect of the drink made him maudlin, never violent, and she had no greater problem with him than that of ensuring he got his boots off before getting into bed.

As to his lateness, she knew exactly what caused it. The policeman, who had lived in the late Victorian house-cum-police-station two hundred yards across the machair from the hotel, had been an islander himself though from one of the Inner isles. He had been nearly twelve years in the posting and had devised a method of saving himself trouble while keeping other people out of it. At nine thirty on a Friday night, always a heavy night down at the bar, he used to put his head in for a few minutes and assess who was likely to be the worse for wear at closing time. Then he would go round the cars that were parked haphazardly on the machair round the hotel and collect ignition keys. No one ever locked their cars on the island or their house doors for that matter.

On emerging into the evening light, supposing it was summer, those who found their cars immobilised would walk down the burn and forgather by the stone bridge that spanned it as it entered the harbour. There, leaning over the parapet, they would continue, as far as they were capable, discussing whatever they had been discussing, supposing anyone could remember what it was. If it was raining or a time of year when darkness had already fallen they would just sit in their cars. In any case it would be a long wait, since there was no point in trying to reclaim their keys from the police house until they could prove they were sober enough to return home without hazard to other road users or inconvenience to the representative of the law.

This system of maintaining safety on the island roads had continued for many years and was accepted by all as just and reasonable. But now changes had come. The policeman had been withdrawn to a new job on the mainland, and a 'bright lad' from East Lothian had taken his place.

The new policeman was instantly unpopular. The cards were stacked against him in any case because he came from the east coast and had no Gaelic. But his arrival was preceded by the rumour that the previous holder of the office had been moved on because he had not been able to log as many arrests per head of the community as those in authority on the mainland required annually. He had 'gone native' they said. Thus the new man was said to have been chosen for his ability to put the average right.

The first mistakes he made were elementary ones. He would introduce himself to complete strangers with a cheery smile and an outstretched hand, saying, 'Hello, I'm Bill Cameron, the new police constable. I don't think we have met. And your name is...?'

People so addressed found it impossible not to reply, 'John Lachy MacLean', or whatever they were called, and thereafter felt like marked men, and went to great lengths to be out if the policeman was coming by, or to disappear behind a building if his car came in sight.

Next, on a visit to the manse, he called the minister's wife 'dear'.

By the time she had recovered herself he had left, so her husband had to bear the brunt of her indignation.

'Dear, indeed! What a nerve! I'll "dear" him if he ever comes near me again, just you wait till…'

'Hush, dear,' said the minister.

'And don't you "dear" me either, my lad, if you know what's good for you,' her voice was rising.

'Sorry, dear – I mean, I'm sorry.'

And so the minister was not very keen on the new man either.

Then the policeman made it very clear to Davy Bell, who ran the hotel, that he would not tolerate drunkenness on *his* patch, and actually asked Davy to give him, in confidence, the names of likely offenders. Or so it was said. At any rate, word of this enormity went round the island like thistle-down in a high wind, and opprobrium of the new policeman and all that pertained to him was universal.

His wife, a shy little woman, had never in her life till now been further from home than Glasgow, nor wanted to. She loathed the island from the moment she first set her high heels on the pier in a November gale and complained to her husband daily. On her only attempt to pull herself together and make friends at a church social she had been reduced to tears by stiff smiles and averted looks.

Soon the iron set into Bill Cameron's soul, and his critics' pre-determined view of him came to be matched by reality.

So Mairi MacPhail's fears as she watched over her oatcakes that July Friday night were very real ones. Two of their neighbours, one admittedly a near-alcoholic, had already lost their licences as a result of Cameron's vengeful diligence. The other had merely

44

been celebrating the birth of his son and needed to drive for his job, poor soul.

Apart from the shame involved, which she would feel very keenly, should Archie suffer the same fate (for he was only, as she put it, an occasional drinker who took no more than a man should) there was the croft to worry about. Three miles of track lay between their croft below Brodach and the main road into Torisay village and the pier. Without the use of the mini-van, for she could not drive herself, how would Archie collect his needs from the agricultural suppliers when they came on the boat? How would she ever do her shopping? And it was nearly two miles to the telephone, supposing they needed the doctor.

She shook her head as she stared into the radiant coals that winked back at her through the bars of the range.

'Oh, Archie,' she sighed aloud, 'just you mind how you go, my lad.'

A thin wisp of black smoke snaked out of the corner of the door of the new electric oven.

It was after ten o'clock when Archie was finally travelling towards home. He had driven less than a couple of miles along the single-track tarmac road before he felt sleep dragging at his eyelids. This was not a usual occurrence when he was driving, for in the balmy days of the old policeman he had been accustomed to spend the two hours between closing time and key-collecting time asleep in the back of his van behind the hotel. Thus he would feel relatively fresh and in control for the drive home. So when his lids began to droop his inclination to repeat his old practice and his memory of Mairi's parting injunction, 'You'll watch out for that Cameron, Archie, and not have any accidents or the like...' combined to make him seek out a place where he could pull his car in off the road.

Every few hundred yards a white marker post indicated a widening of the tarmac on one or other side where cars could overtake or pass each other. Into one of these havens Archie manoeuvred his little van, not without difficulty, until he was satisfied that, though at an unusual angle, he could be causing no possible obstruction.

Then, settling himself low in his seat and pulling his cap down over his eyes, he prepared for slumber. In the back of the van, Meg, who knew the form, trampled a round dent into a pile of sacking and with a contented sigh curled herself neatly into a ball and tucked her nose under her feathered black tail.

A roar that Archie at first thought was a tidal wave, which made sense in the context of his dream, woke him with a jerk. Sliding his cap up he was then aware in his rear-view mirror of two red lights disappearing over the rise in the road behind him with, above and between them, a flashing blue one. He was shocked into lucidity and awareness. That was Cameron going by and he could not have failed to see the parked van and he would be back, if only out of curiosity. He would have to go on to the next passing place to turn, which gave Archie about a minute and a half to assess and deal with the situation.

He reached for his ignition key. No, to drive away now would be madness. The one thing he shouldn't be doing was driving. A thought struck him. He opened the van door.

'Meg, here now, quick, over here.'

He fumbled at her collar.

'Here you are, then, good lass. Away home now. On ye go, away home to Mairi, away home!'

Without hesitation the little collie streaked across the road and over the low wall. As Archie shut the door he could just see the white tip at the end of her tail as she ran low and swift into the gloom that hid the field and the hill beyond. She would cross the bog and get home the short way. Then Archie and the van were caught in the full glare of the headlights coming over the rise. The big police Land Rover pulled in behind him, a door shut,

46

and he heard the measured tread of approaching boots.

'Get out of your car, please,' said Bill Cameron's east coast voice.

Archie swayed slightly and steadied himself on the car door, screwing up his face and blinking at the torchlight shining into his eyes.

'Good evening, Mr Cameron,' he said.

'Well, well. So it's Archie MacPhail, is it?'

There was no attempt to conceal the triumph in the policeman's voice.

It was nearly midnight when Mairi saw the lights bumping down the track and she could tell that they belonged to a larger vehicle than Archie's van. She had been aching with worry for some time. The arrival of the dog, exhausted as she was and with the white of her legs stained brown with bog water, had done nothing to relieve her fears. Closer inspection had only added an element of mystification.

By the time the policeman was knocking on the door her hair was neat and tidy and she appeared totally composed as she opened it.

'Good evening, Mrs MacPhail.'

Mairi nodded, standing with her hand on the door latch, allowing him into the porch, but no further.

'I would not be bothering you with such a late call if you had taken the precaution to install a telephone, so you'll excuse the intrusion.'

She nodded again, hardly taking in what he was saying. He was smiling, so Archie had not had an accident, she thought.

'You'll know very well where your husband has been tonight,' said Cameron, 'but I thought I had better let you know where he is now, in case you were wondering. He's in the cell at the police station, and he'll stay there until he's sober enough in the morning to hear the charge he will be facing.'

'What is this you are telling me?' Mairi was very still, only the tips of her fingers moving at the edge of her apron. Her voice displayed no emotion whatever, and there was a steely ring to its monotonal quality.

'Tomorrow he will be formally charged with being drunk in charge of a motor vehicle.'

'My husband is a respectable man,' said Mairi, her chin rising. 'He has never been in a police cell in his life. I will not believe you.'

'Maybe you won't, Mrs MacPhail,' said the policeman, 'but it will not make any difference. Anyway, I have satisfied the requirements by telling you.'

He turned to leave, bending his head to pass under the door frame. Then, with an afterthought, he stepped back in again.

'He had a grand story to tell me, though. He said he hadn't been driving at all! He said he's left the car there in the morning and got a lift home. Then he got another lift down to the hotel in the evening and he left his car key here in the house. He told me he just stopped by his car for a *wee sleep*! Does he think I'm daft, to believe that kind of rubbish? They'll try anything on…'

A shaft of light shot through Mairi's brain. For a moment she stared at the sneering policeman, then she moved to reach for the hook behind the door. She faced him again.

'Well, maybe *you* will believe *this*, Mister Police Constable Cameron. I will have you know,' the voice was rising but the words were slow and deliberate, 'that my husband has never been drunk in charge of anything. Here is his car key and here is where it has been all this day. And Mr MacBride that sold him the car last year, he will tell you there is just the one key, and maybe you will believe *him*.'

PC Cameron, confronted by a figure that looked each moment more like Boadicea at the reins of her chariot, with the key being shaken within an inch of his nose, backed out of the doorway, bumping his head on the lintel and losing his cap, which he had omitted to remove on entry. Helped by a wanton gust of wind it rolled unevenly down the slight slope from the doorstep, and the policeman was forced to follow it at an ungainly stoop and finally stop it with his foot.

'And another thing, Bill Cameron,' called Mairi after him, the fire in her belly now a raging furnace, 'a letter, a report of this incident will be going to your superiors, so it will. Fancy putting a respectable man like Archie in prison, my goodness!'

She collapsed in tears as soon as the fugitive tail lights were out of sight down the track. But by the time the police Rover re-appeared three quarters of an hour later all traces of her emotion had vanished. The kettle was singing on the range.

Archie sat in his usual chair with a cup of tea in his hands and smiled as Mairi repeated again the words of her final sally.

He did not look at her, finding a certain difficulty in meeting his wife's eye. With his foot he fondled the little collie lying on the floor in front of him, flat out in her sleep.

'You are a good lass,' he said, nodding. 'You did well tonight, right enough. I'm proud of the two of you.'

Mairi turned to the range, blushing slightly, understanding, and happy in her share of the praise.

BESSIE

1970s

'Here we are then!' The nurse's brisk and cheerful voice roused Bessie from her semi-doze. The bustling pink-striped movements stirred the still air of the room into whirling eddies of bright competence. Bessie screwed up her eyes in an effort to shut out the sound and drift back into darkness, but it was not allowed.

'Come on, now, Bessie, if we sleep all day what are we going to do tonight? We'll away out dancing, is that it? I'm sure you were a great dancer, with your neat wee feet.' She pulled the bed table near to where Bessie lay and placed a tray on it.

'We've got something special for you today, look, one of your favourites: risotto and carrots, and prunes to follow. You'll enjoy that, won't you, dear? There now, shall we bring you up just a wee bit higher? That's better, isn't it? Are you comfy, now? Just look at your hair! Oh dear me, we'll have to make you beautiful before your boyfriend comes to see you, will we not? We can't have him seeing you looking all rag, tag and bobtail.'

The girl's quick movements and pattering talk made Bessie feel confused. She waited for a pause before saying what she had been waiting to say all through the quiet morning.

'Nurse, I want to go home.'

The nurse stirred the food on the plate, blending it all together, and taking some of it on the tip of the spoon, blew on it. Then she touched it with the back of one of her well-scrubbed fingers.

'That's just nice,' she said. 'Open, then, and pop it in. Is that good?'

Bessie swallowed obediently and tried again.

'Nurse, I want to go home.'

The nurse talked on, spoon in hand, her eyes moving occasionally to the door, expectant.

'Come on now, dear, another wee spoonful … o-ooh, that's lovely.'

'Nurse, I want to…' Bessie began.

'Oh, look, now, what we've done…' she clicked her tongue, and reached for the big box of paper tissues on the bedside table. 'All down your front, on your nice clean nightie. Oh, dear me. Well, never you mind, we'll get you all cleaned up in a minute. Try again, now … tha-a-at's better.'

She opened her own mouth a little each time as if to encourage her patient. To humour her, to make her listen, Bessie accepted several small mouthfuls, and then shook her head.

'Come on, dear,' the nurse coaxed, 'just a wee bit more. To bring the roses to your cheeks.'

Bessie pushed the spoon away, catching sight as she did so of the shiny blue raised veins criss-crossing the back of her hand like so many little mountain ranges. Tiny brown blots lay in the valleys between. Her hands often seemed unfamiliar, as if they belonged to someone else, and she always felt surprised they were not smooth and rounded with neat narrow fingers as she felt them to be. She seized her opportunity as the nurse turned briefly away, and said again, more firmly,

'I want to go home.'

'Are you wanting to say something, dear? Are you ready for your prunes? They look lovely, and we've got custard on them today.'

Bessie wanted to say she hated custard, that she had always hated custard, she had hated it when she was a child, but she knew the nurse would not understand, so she just turned her head from side to side, avoiding the spoon. A blob of custard fell on her chin and she closed her eyes in revulsion as she smelt its cloying sweetness.

'Come on now, dear,' said the nurse, 'that's naughty. What am I going to say to the doctor when he asks if you've been a good girl? Am I going to tell him you won't eat your nice dinner? He'll not be pleased with you. Just a wee try, now.'

'Tell the doctor I want to go home,' said Bessie.

'That's better, in it goes … there, that's not so bad, is it? Are we going to have another?'

Bessie turned her head wearily against the pillow and the drip of custard picked up a long wisp of grey hair.

The nurse sighed. They were hard to nurse, these stroke patients. As she wiped the soft creased skin with a tissue she once again had the impression the older woman was struggling to speak. It was sad, really, there was no voice there now. They did sometimes get to speak again though.

At the sound of footsteps in the passage her movements quickened. She removed the tray and smoothed the bed sheet tight round the frail body.

'There now, there's your boyfriend coming and we're not ready, are we? Never mind. Good afternoon, doctor. Here we are, all ready for you, but we're still not eating very well, I'm afraid. Bessie's taken a scunner to her prunes, and she should have them.'

The doctor looked down at Bessie for a moment, frowning.

He walked over to the window and stood looking out at the rain falling on the grey slate roofs below. As he turned again towards the bed his head brushed the long fronds of fern trailing down from a crocheted basket hanging from the ceiling hook in front of the window. It was the only live thing in Bessie's room and she liked to see it swaying as it was now.

'We thought bringing her up here would get her eating better.' He sounded concerned. 'Some of them can't take the wards and the communal rooms and last week I thought that was what was wrong here. It's hard to tell. Maybe I was wrong. At least they keep each other company down there, even if they can't communicate, most of them. We'll have to have a rethink here. We'll see how she is in a day or two.'

Bessie gathered up all her energy and said, 'Doctor, I want to go home. I must go home.'

'She's not strong,' said the nurse, 'and I don't know how long she could sit up in a chair, now. But she never looked happy downstairs.'

'Oh, dear God, will you not listen to me?' said Bessie. 'I want to go home. I don't want to die in this place. I must get back home.'

'I sometimes think she is trying to speak,' said the nurse.

'Well,' said the doctor, 'there's no real reason she shouldn't speak. Anyway, we'll try and stimulate that appetite a bit and then see how we get on. I think she's better in her own room really. Does she watch the box at all?'

They looked at the dead grey eye of the television set squatting silently on a bracket attached to the wall. The nurse shook her head and followed him out of the room.

As the door closed Bessie felt tears welling up in her eyes. She had placed so much faith in the doctor. Up till now he had always seemed to understand what she needed. It was he who had rescued her from the hell of her days in the communal day room. He had stood in front of her chair the day she was scream-ing and through her screams she had heard him say,

'Bessie doesn't seem so happy today. Are you trying to tell me something, Bessie? Is it the TV you don't like? Would you like to be nearer the window?'

She had tried to tell him how she felt and he seemed to under-stand. I am going mad, she said; unless you take me away from this place, I know I will go off my head. I cannot stand the smell in this room – can you not smell it, the stale urine? There is hardly a soul in this circle of chairs who is still continent. And do you not see the shaking, gaping faces, the drooling mouths? Can you not hear the endless, meaningless, muttering and moaning? Half of these people have no idea whether they are asleep or awake, alive or dead; they just sit staring at the television and they will not even notice when the nurses turn it off. They are all just sitting there, mouldering, waiting to die, and they are beyond caring when it happens. And they have put me in here to die with them. It's not the dying I mind, but I will *not* die here with them. You must, oh dear God, you must take me out of here, please take me out of here…

And the doctor had understood and had her moved to a room of her own. But now even he was no longer listening to her and the smell of death was creeping into this room too.

She was appalled by her helplessness. She felt that as the days went by all her determination was slipping away. There were moments, like now, when she could not stand what was hap-pening to her any longer and she knew she must act. But even while she was thinking about it a lassitude would creep over her and though she knew she meant to do something important she would forget what it was. Then she would lie weeping silently like a child, her tears coursing down her cheeks and her mind aching with self-pity.

But today, despite her tiredness, her thoughts were clearer.

Home, that was what she wanted. If she could keep her mind firmly on that, she might finally be able to make something happen. She needed to go home. This place, here, was where her problems were. At home everything would be all right. Last time she had had a visitor from the island, Jenny Campbell it was, she had said her house was just fine and the neighbours were keeping her cat fed. They were missing her on the island, Jenny said.

Well, no one could stop her, could they, if she wanted to go? This was not a prison. She had come here of her own free will and she was as free to leave. She could get up and go home if she wanted to. Well, why not? She had never really thought about it like that before. She would go home now.

Her coat was hanging in the wardrobe and she pulled it on with no trouble over her blue viyella nightdress. It was warm and familiar and on the lapel was pinned a little carved wooden edelweiss which had been there for so many years. One of her boys had brought it back to her from Switzerland.

She passed along the empty corridor, her thick bedroom slippers with their leather soles and woolly pom-poms making no sound on the shiny vinyl floor. The swing doors closed silently after her. She met no one.

'I am lucky,' she thought, 'they are still at their dinner.'

In the road outside a bus was just pulling up. She climbed on board and sat in the nearest seat.

'Five pence it is to the pier,' the conductor spoke in a familiar West Highland voice. It was a change after the Glasgow accents which had surrounded her recently and she found it comforting. She said to him in Gaelic that it was a lovely day and he replied in the familiar language that indeed it was.

The mail-boat was moored to one of the heavy bollards which stood at intervals along the heavy wooden baulks of the pier. The harbour water glittered between the gaps in the wood and she remembered how, as a child, she had stumbled and dropped one of her two pennies of pocket money down between them and heard the tiny 'plop' as it hit the water.

'That will teach you a lesson, Bessie,' her mother had said. 'That penny was for the plate on Sunday and now you will have to put in your spending penny instead. Another time you'll do as I say and keep your pennies inside your glove.'

Her mother never met a bad situation without thinking of a way to make it worse. Bessie remembered, also, her father's wink as he slipped another penny into her hand on the way to the church that Sunday.

These thoughts reminded her that she had no money now for the fare. She would have to explain the situation to Johnnie McRae the Purser, who would surely understand her predicament. He was a good lad, Johnnie. They had been in school together.

Bessie climbed the steeply sloping gang-plank, gripping the wooden rail, and walked along the desk to the little cupboard from which Johnnie dispensed tickets. She was surprised to see it was not Johnnie McRae sitting there, but young Alec MacBride, whose father had the hotel in Torisay. He was not yet thirteen years old, she could swear.

'What are you doing here, Alec, on a Monday? You should be in school.'

'It's not Monday, Miss MacIlwraith, and it's the holidays, anyway.'

She had forgotten, and to hide her lapse of memory she lifted the tide table from the desk in front of him and said, 'Don't tell me you can make sense of that, Alec MacBride, or you've changed since you were in my class.'

'You won't tell on me, Miss MacIlwraith?'

'I'll not tell on you, Alec, but I will see you later.'

The boat was moving, smoke belching from the funnel, the timbers juddering as the engine rumbled away in its depth. Bessie walked along the gently heaving deck to one of the slatted bench seats on the foredeck, the kind that turns into a life-raft in the event of a shipwreck. But these little ships that did the island mail run were well suited to the Hebridean waters and it was many years since one had gone down. Bessie's father had been on board, on that occasion, returning from conducting a funeral service on a neighbouring island where there had been no Baptist minister and he was required to officiate. There had been few survivors and he had not been among them.

Bessie sat with her eyes turned towards the islands in the distance, knowing each by the rounded humps which slowly rose into view as the boat travelled over the curve of the water. From a distance there always seemed to be a great many islands, more than there should be, but as the horizon sank the humps linked up and were revealed as hill tops, three or four to an island.

There were two calls to be made before they arrived at Bessie's destination. The first was short, a pause at another smaller wooden pier where the mail bag was hurled into the air and landed with a dull thump on the wet logs. It was lifted by a small boy who threw it across his shoulder.

'Nothing to go,' he called.

Then he ran with it to where his father waited, holding a red-painted bicycle with a big basket fixed to the handlebars. He waved to the captain as he stood on the bridge but his cry of greeting was drowned by the sound of the propellers as the boat backed away.

At the next island they spent longer, for there were a dozen heifers to be unloaded, and as many passengers. There was no pier here and a long open boat came out from the shore rowed by two men who, without even looking over their shoulders, came unerringly to the side of the mail-boat.

The passengers climbed down the ladder to be ferried ashore first, and then the rowers returned for the cattle. Each in turn was released from the pen in the hold and lifted and swung down by the small deck crane into the open boat. Their stomachs were supported by the canvas cradle, their legs dangling pathetically and their heads hanging mournfully down towards the out-stretched hands below. With five beasts on board the rowers set off again. Halfway to the shore one frightened young cow leapt overboard and completed the journey swimming. Two collie dogs greeted it with excited barks and herded it dripping towards the huddle of its companions.

When they were all ashore the foghorn of the mail-boat emitted two short blasts. After a few moments a small procession moved slowly towards the shore from the back of a building a few hundred yards up the track. The mourners were all male, all dressed in dark suits and all wearing high-crowned bowler hats. Six of them shouldered a pale new coffin which they loaded into the long boat.

'Who is it?' whispered Bessie to the young seaman who was standing beside her at the rail, his cap in his hand.

'Do you not know?' he looked at her curiously. 'He was from Torisay, and they are taking him home now. He was the Baptist minister.'

He turned away to help lift the coffin on board. Bessie stood with her head bowed as it was carried past her along the deck to where it would travel in the solitary state of the only cabin on the boat.

As they approached Torisay pier an hour later Bessie felt a rising sense of excitement. The late afternoon sun was casting a golden light on the slope of the hill which rose at the back of the village, no more than a mile away. The light dusting of heather upon it glowed purple and Bessie knew it was alive and humming with bees. When she was a child, her father had shown her how to trick the wild bees into giving up their honey. In May time she had helped him to dig shallow holes in the turf of the field set aside for hay, filling each with a little dry grass. They would cover the holes with flat stones and then make sloping entrance tunnels by pushing a piece of piping in the yielding sandy soil. With the pipe pulled out, the warm holes became just the kind of place bees love to make their nests. The entrances would be concealed by the growing grass, and all summer long the bees would come and go laden with the pollen from the wildflowers which grew like scattered confetti on the machair, and from the heather as it came into bloom on the slopes above. When the hay was cut in August, and the stones were lifted, some of the holes would yield a rich golden harvest.

Bessie savoured still the distinctive scent and the tangy taste on her tongue of the sweet heather honey.

'That's a grand haul you have there,' her mother would say, approving for once, and pleased to receive the bucket of lumpy brown honeycomb. She would dismiss with little sympathy the odd bee sting – 'nothing good came without pain' – directing the sufferer to the tin of soothing bicarbonate of soda which stood by the range, ready for making girdle scones. For three or four days a jelly bag would hang from a low beam while the pure gold honey would ooze drip by drip into the enamel bowl below.

A small cluster of folk stood on the pier awaiting the boat, taking the opportunity of gathering news and passing messages. People from different parts of the island who never met from one month to the next greeted each other warmly and took up conversations from previous occasions. Meeting the weekly boat was always a very social event, and some folk wore their Sunday clothes.

Bessie saw one or two parents of erstwhile pupils who she would like to have a word with, but they were deep in talk, and seemed not to notice her.

Then she caught sight of a figure beckoning to her from the pier head. It was Colin Lamont, standing by that old dog-cart of his, holding the reins at the head of a little dun Highland garron.

'Hullo, Bessie,' he called. 'Is that you off the boat? You'll be wanting a ride home. If you can come now I will take you.'

'That will do fine, Colin,' she replied. 'But surely it is out of your way?'

'Your way is my way, Bessie.' He helped her in. 'And it always has been, except you would never make up your mind.'

'Och, you, Colin Lamont, you never change.'

She was pleased, although she knew she would never take him seriously. He was looking at her bedroom slippers as he settled her in to the seat, but he was far too polite to make any comment. She pulled her coat together over her knees where the blue viyella was showing.

The pony, knowing it had turned for home, threw all its weight into the collar and trotted steadily up the track to the village. As they passed the harbour Bessie saw the small clinker-built boats lying on the sand, stranded by the receding tide, their running ropes swooping from wall ring, to boat, to sunken mooring. A coal 'puffer' was tied to the old stone jetty. It sat high in the remaining water, so it must have done its trip round the coastline, unloading orders of coal at various landing points to be collected by the different crofters who had chartered it. The crew would be relaxing in the bar of the hotel, or visiting friends on the island, having a dram here and there. In the morning, while it was still dark, they would start the long trip back to Ayrshire for another load. The course steered out of the harbour would depend on the hospitality the captain had received.

They passed through the village without talking, Colin intent on steering his enthusiastic pony, Bessie enjoying every aspect of the place she loved. There was not an inch of this island that was not familiar to her, and as they drew near to the land of her father's croft she felt like someone who has been long cold nearing a warm and welcoming fire.

The track, which was now no more than worn wheel marks

on the machair, rolled on over the gently undulating ground. The going was as smooth as velvet, the cart only deviating from a straight line to avoid the odd rock, a clump of marram grass or the slope of a steeper sand dune. Small groups of sheep gazed ruminatively at them as they passed, and a long-legged hare loped easily in front of them until it turned away up a sand gully. The whistling siren trill of a whaup sounded nearby, and two of the leggy, curved-beaked birds rose into the air at the sight of the pony and cart.

Each rise and fall of the land was dear to Bessie and achingly familiar. She knew the name of every one of the flowers scattered on the machair with such a profligate hand. Her happiest memories were of bringing her class down to the dunes on fine days, teaching the children some of these things she felt she had been born knowing.

She felt her heart beating faster, as they approached the last rise when the croft house where she was born would come into view. She could hear the doctor's words in her ears, warning against 'over-excitement'. She would give that doctor excitement if he were here with her now. This kind of excitement was what she needed as a thirsty soul needs water. The little gelding slowed as they went up and then came gently over the top of the rise.

There it was, her home, the little thatched croft house nestling in the shelter of an encircling arm of rock, gleaming white in the sunlight with a new coat of lime, a thin drift of smoke rising from the central chimney in the thatch.

There was a narrow burn crossed by a small arched stone bridge. Just below the bridge the burn widened, the result of generations of digging by Bessie's family, into a small pond of shallow brown peaty water.

The feeling of joy was now such a positive ache that she felt almost like crying out.

'Stop here, Colin, and let me down. I would like to walk.'

With an effort she pulled herself forward in the seat, and laboriously moved her legs round until her feet were touching the ground. Her body was enormously heavy, as if the cart were holding her back, and her legs, as she put her weight onto them, felt strange and distant. She steadied herself by holding the side of the cart and feasted her eyes on the sight in front of her.

A little convoy of ducks moved out from under the bank of the pond, the drake in the lead and his mate half a length behind. In the V-shaped ripple they left, five tiny ducklings paddled frantically, little balls of fluff, brown streaked with yellow, hardly marking the water as they skittered over it. Bessie smiled; there had always been duck on the pond and this must be an early brood.

Her eyes and her heart moved over the water to the house. It stood half-facing into the sun, its back to the rock, one shoulder towards the sea, on its little surrounding frill of grey pebbles from the shore; the thatch of its roof seemed as ever to be the home of countless small birds; and the grey tabby cat, Bessie's own kitten now grown with kittens of her own, lay outstretched on the four-foot-deep sill of the window, one long leg hanging languidly down.

She saw quite close to her the clean linen, shirts and long 'combinations', hanging on the washing line and moving lightly in the breeze. She heard whistling and the clanking of milk pails from the steadings alongside the house. The top half of her mother's front door stood open and her nostrils filled with the evocative smell of fresh baking.

She took a step forward and swayed dizzily. Where was Colin? Could he not give her a hand? How was she to walk to the house when her limbs seemed unable to obey her? She must get there, after coming all this way. She had to get there. One step, then another. Through misty eyes she saw a figure at the door of the byre, and she heard her father's voice.

'Is that you home, Bessie?'

She looked down at her slippers inching their way slowly across the ground, but as she raised her eyes again the whole scene seemed to sway and swing in front of her. She grasped for support at the long ribbon of green lace hanging from the washing line over her head, but she still lost her balance and stumbled forward. For a second or two the lace held, but then came away, and with it still clutched in her hand Bessie slid to the ground.

The nurse said to the sister, 'I just heard this crash and I came running in. She was lying over there by the window with that plant on top of her and soil all over the place. I could see at once she was gone.'

'Poor old thing,' said the sister. 'It'll be her heart this time, I expect he'll say. It just beats me how she managed to get as far as that – she hasn't been on her feet for months, just in the wheel-chair. There's more determination in some of these old people than you think.'

'Poor soul…' the nurse sighed. 'I wonder what made her do it? I wonder where she thought she was going?'

Then she got down on her knees with the dustpan and brush.

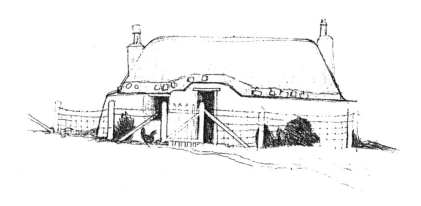

DOUGIE BĀN

1980s

Dougie MacLean, or Dougie Bān, so called because of his shock of flaxen hair, had time for everyone. No one ever came to him with a request and had it refused.

'No, no, no,' he would say, 'my tea can wait. Just you show me the wheel, and I'll get it fixed for you in no time at all.'

He would drop whatever he was doing to help anyone with anything at any time of day or night, and everyone knew it. So everyone said to everyone else, 'Ask Dougie Bān. He'll do it for you.' And they did, and he did.

The door of his small black-house on the edge of the village stood permanently open, an invitation to passers-by. In fact it wouldn't shut properly anyway, because the day Dougie was re-fixing the door frame someone came to ask him if he could spare an hour or two with his tractor to pull something out of a ditch, and Dougie had left a small pile of newly mixed cement on the doorstep. Many hours later it had hardened irrevocably and Dougie hadn't yet found time to chip it off. The rest of the cement was still just outside the door, a bag-shaped grey sculpture, because during those hours it had also rained hard. Sometimes Dougie Bàn sat on it with a mug of tea in his hand.

His life was odd jobs. Odd jobs for everybody – that was Dougie. The funny thing was that he was not in it for the money.

'Dougie, how much do I owe you?' they would plead. But he would do anything to avoid taking payment.

'Not a thing, nothing at all, seeing it's you,' he would say, and change the subject. That was with his friends. With strangers he would just look uncomfortable, and with his eyes fidgeting along the horizon he would say, 'Ah well, I'll have to work it out. I'll let you know.'

And they would not hear from him again.

Some people, if they bothered to wonder at Dougie's uncharging helpfulness to all and sundry, assumed he had 'money tucked away', or he was on some kind of social security fiddle. Others, more charitable, thought he was probably illiterate, certainly simple, and just couldn't cope with handling cash. 'But he seems to get along somehow.'

Others again, who had perhaps subconsciously guessed at the truth, paid Dougie Bàn for his services anonymously and in kind. A bag of turnips left against the wall of the house; a bottle of whisky slipped under the seat of his van; or a sweater hand-knitted from wool unravelled from the children's outgrown jerseys. And then there was the oblique approach:

'Dougie, do you know anyone who could give our old cooker a home? It works fine, but the wife wants a new one. Can you get rid of it for me?'

The fact was his needs were simple. He lived on his own, no wife, no mortgage. He had a milking cow, and he grew his own potatoes in a lazybed behind the house, some cabbages and onions. He didn't need to add much for a good meal once a day, and for the rest, well, bread, cheese and gooseberry jam went a long way. And of course he fished.

The wonder was that he ever got anything done at home, for he always allowed himself to be interrupted if he had started a job.

'Dougie, have you a minute? My drain's blocked, and the plumber's off the island.'

He always had a minute, and he had it now, not tomorrow, not next week, like everyone else. He had always been the same. Before he left Torisay school old Bessie MacIlwraith, the head teacher, had said of him, 'Dougie Bān will never finish anything if there is something else he can start first.' She had hit on an interesting truth, but not the whole of it. Simple he might be, she said, even a little retarded, but definitely not mental. Slow, yes, but it was the slowness of deliberation, of intent. He knew what he was doing.

But even the perceptive Miss MacIlwraith never discovered Dougie's secret. Everybody knew Dougie Bān, but nobody knew his secret. Nobody even guessed he had a secret, and nobody would have believed it if they had been told what it was.

The fact is, Dougie Bān believed he was a saint. Not just a good man, a righteous upright member of the community, though he tried to be that as well. But a fully-fledged, biblically qualified saint. Saint Dougal. Saint Dougal of Torisay, perhaps, or of the Outer Isles – history would give him a full title in time.

It had all come about many years earlier, perhaps thirty-three years ago. He had been about eight, or nine, still at primary school. A trip had been arranged for his class to go to Glasgow, to visit the circus. It was a three-day excursion – four hours on the ferry to the mainland, fish and chips for dinner near the pier, and then the bus (except they called it a coach, with all its royal overtones) for a long, long drive down the coast, then the twisty road along Loch Lomond-side and finally into Glasgow. That night was spent in accommodation provided by the Youth

Hostels Association, two long rooms lined with single beds, one room for the boys and the other for the girls. The excitement was tangible. Most of the children were on their first visit to Glasgow, and for some, like Dougie, it was their first trip off the island. Sleep came late and short. Three times during the night Miss MacIlwraith warned that if she had to come in once again it would be no circus and straight home in the morning.

The next afternoon they had to catch an ordinary street bus out to the circus and this was when it all went wrong. The first bus had only eight free seats, and the school party had to split in two, half with each of the two teachers. Dougie heard his name called by Miss MacIlwraith as she ran to the second bus. Then he heard his name called again, and turned back to the first one. Somehow, in the confusion he managed to miss both buses, but hearing the fading voice of Miss MacIlwraith shouting, 'The next bus, Dougie, take the next bus!' he used his initiative and got onto the third bus which had pulled in behind.

Dougie was not frightened. He had no doubt his bus would get him to the circus, and when he saw a huge tent set back on an open space near the road he got out at the next stop and started towards it, following the crowd, and keeping a look-out for his companions.

No one asked him for a ticket at the entrance, and as the place was very crowded he took the first free seat he found, at the end of a row very near the front.

He was surprised when they all started singing a hymn, but he had never been to a circus before, and life, especially in Glasgow, was full of surprises. He sang with the rest from a sheet, and then listened in astonishment to speeches which made even the most heated sermons from the Torisay pulpit seem like nursery rhymes. People spoke of sin and shame, of retribution, of terror and of joy. Some cried out and tore their clothes and one man lay on his face weeping in the gangway only a few feet away from Dougie.

Dougie Bān was transfixed, in fascination and embarrassment. The music got louder and curtains opened at the back of the stage to reveal a man in a pale suit and a colourful tie who walked slowly down to near where Dougie sat. He stopped only a few feet away and spoke. His voice, quiet and compelling, with a strange accent, seemed to come from every corner of the huge tent. He spoke of God's love and forgiveness and of how with God's love there was nothing you could not do. Through God's love even the blackest sinner could become as white as snow. Dougie believed him – it was hard not to believe this man with the piercing eyes and persuasive voice.

'God is calling you, calling you now!' His voice was rising. 'You can hear the voice of God calling, calling your name. Come, come, he is saying, now, at this moment, now, come, leave your seat and come…'

He beckoned with his arms and Dougie found he had risen from his seat and was climbing the steps onto the platform. He heard other footsteps behind him, but he could not take his eyes from the man, who took him by the hand.

'This innocent child,' (the man was now trembling with emotion) 'is the first to answer God's call. I tell you all,' (his voice rose to a penetrating bugle pitch) 'this child has ears open to the voice of God, and with those ears ever open he will become one of God's holy saints, and dwell forever in the temple of the Lord. Come, I say unto you, come! God is calling you – now!'

The man dropped Dougie's hand, and Dougie still stood in front of him, gazing up at him. The man gave his shoulder a slight push, and spoke quietly. 'Through the curtains at the back, sonny – one of the guardians will take your details. They'll tell you what to do.'

Dougie walked half-dazed through the gap in the curtains, and a girl with a ribbon saying 'I answered God's call' slung across her bosom got up from a canvas chair and called, 'Kevin, they're coming through.'

'Christ, it's babies now. What next?' The man beside her stubbed out his cigarette.

'Hush, you,' she said. 'I'll do this. Hello, and what's your name, then?'

'Dougie. He said you would tell me what to do.'

'Well, you're to be a good boy, Dougie and – and – do everything you're told right away, and be helpful and that. Eh – do you want to give me your name and address?'

'Christ,' said the man again.

'Pardon?'

'Do you want to buy "The Way to Salvation"?'

'I haven't any money, I'm sorry.'

'Never you worry,' said the girl kindly. 'Away home with you, and just do what I said. Peace be with you, friend.'

She was speaking now to a woman who was crying quietly in the doorway.

Dougie walked out of a gap in the tent marked EXIT and found himself in brilliant daylight, which made him blink. Hours later he had somehow found his way back to the Youth Hostel and a furious Miss MacIlwraith.

'Dougie MacLean, if ever I take you anywhere ever again… Thank God you're back. I've just about… Get you on up to your bed. That's enough of you today.'

Dougie didn't mind. He had a lot of thinking to do.

From that day his difficult destiny was never far from his thoughts. His main worry was how he would live up to the expectations of the man in the tent. The instructions were fairly simple. Being good was not something he found hard, since he was naturally neither naughty nor rebellious. And doing everything he was asked right away was not difficult as long as he remembered. The only problem was when his Auntie Jean asked him to do one thing and his uncle John-Lachy asked him to do another when he hadn't finished the first task and Auntie Jean then called him again from the kitchen. But he accommodated this problem by simply always responding at once to the latest request, and those who knew him well adapted accordingly.

'Don't you dare tell Dougie to get the milk till he's done washing down the tractor.'

They looked at him as 'a funny wee boy' but very handy around the place. Certainly he amply repaid the generosity with which they had taken him in as a 'boarded out' when he was a toddler, when his own parents had been unable to cope with their large family. To all intents and purposes John-Lachy and Jean MacLean saw him as an extra son, their own family being long grown, and likely to be less trouble as he grew older than a more normal boy.

At school it was harder, and he gained the reputation for being a dreamer. Actually he was just thinking a great deal about how to cope with the different demands made on him by teachers and friends.

Dougie Bān became noticeable for the regularity of his attendance at the Sunday School. His aunt proudly spread the line of his certificates along the shelf of the kitchen dresser, with 'Dougald MacLean' in neat sloping writing on the dotted line on each. Reading was difficult for him, so the Sunday School teacher was patient and understanding (though rather surprised) as week after week he re-borrowed 'Lives of the Saints told to the Children'. He discovered that very few were saints in their lifetime. Those who were, were called so by others: they didn't regard themselves as saints, which would have been very unsaintly. Humility was the great thing, and living frugally, though often not until after achieving sainthood. This was good, because Dougie enjoyed his food, and he was growing fast.

Many times he wished he had asked in the Tent how long it would take him to become a saint, and how he would actually know when it had happened. Did it happen overnight, or was it a progressive thing?

This awkward question was answered for him when he was about twenty-two. In his usual way he had turned up at the pier to help anyone who might need a hand getting off the boat or getting to wherever they were going. He had his uncle John-Lachy's van, as he had brought down a load of lambs which were going off to the mainland. For the third year running he gave a lift to the English couple and their small children who had a holiday house at the north end of the island. They tried to pay him for his petrol; they asked him in for a cup of tea, 'or a dram, perhaps?' but he refused politely. He returned briefly to the house with something they had left behind in the van, and unintentionally overheard the wife saying to the husband, 'No, I offered, but he wouldn't take a thing… He never does. He's a saint…'

Dougie Bān drove away feeling dizzy with shock. It had happened at last, without him noticing! As soon as he was out of sight he stopped the van and got out. He sat down on a green knoll facing the sea and thought about it. So that was the way of it. You became a saint without realising it, but other people could tell, and this was how you found out. It was just as well he had heard the remark, because now he must start fasting and praying, which was the one thing all saints seemed to do. He couldn't tell anyone, of course, because of humility.

He surprised his aunt by refusing second helpings, and she thought he must be in love. He surprised his uncle by stopping the tractor every hour or so and sitting for a few minutes with his eyes shut. His uncle was an unimaginative man, and thought he was probably suffering, as he did himself, from dyspepsia.

The praying, Dougie found really hard. Eventually he gave it up, because one thing he had learned from his enquiries was that no two saints are alike. They all had their specialities, and he decided his speciality would be no prayers. The rest he would stick to. As the expectation of his stomach declined, he found it easier to eat less and less, and, though he lost a lot of weight, he felt fit, and looked well. He had probably been eating too much for years, anyway, he thought.

For the rest, he had only to go on in a way of life which was admirably suited to his temperament. He was kind and helpful to all, responded to anyone's request for help, and never had to go on with anyone's job if another one intervened, since he always felt constrained, as a good saint, to respond at once to anyone's plea. So he seldom had to do anything to the point where it became tedious.

There was probably never a happier saint in Christendom than Dougie MacLean, nor one more perfectly suited to his role.

When his aunt and uncle died he grieved, as he was truly fond of them. But it solved the problem of receiving alms. It had always concerned him that he had so often to do the shopping in the general stores in Torisay, and he had never before heard of a saint who handled money, except to give it away. From now on, his shopping would be minimal, and he could honourably accept gifts.

The croft on which he had worked for so many years was left to his first cousin, but Dougie Bān was left the small black-house and a walled quarter of an acre of machair on the edge of Torisay. It was not quite a hermit's cell, but with its thick white walls and deep black tarred felt roof it was simple and all he needed.

There was only one thing missing from his life, but he didn't want to risk his humility by bringing it about artificially. Once, when he had brought back to life a car which had been condemned as defunct by both the island garages, someone had said, 'That's a miracle!' But Dougie knew it wasn't. It was just a loosening of a screw head stuck in behind the crank-shaft. He had a feeling, though, that when the moment came, and a real miracle happened, he would know.

Then, one day, when he was in his early forties, he was taking a short-cut in his van across the great beach. The tide had only turned to come in an hour before, and you could save a good half mile by leaving the road and there was fine firm going by the water's edge.

The huge curve of pale sand was unbroken save for a tiny knot of people way down the beach at the edge of the surf about a quarter of a mile short of the far end of the bay. From their brightly-coloured clothes he knew they were trippers, and as he drew closer he recognised the family who had come off the boat at the beginning of the week and were staying in May MacFarlane's guesthouse. They were standing looking out into the bay at a child's red inflatable plastic boat which was drifting out to sea about a hundred yards offshore.

As Dougie pulled up his van beside them, faces of distress were turned towards him and he saw the smallest child was in paroxysms of sobs, her face red and shiny with tears. He thought the grief was rather overdone in view of the nature of the calamity but, ever kind and helpful, he said,

'Have you lost your wee boat, then? Never you mind. I know where I can get you another.'

'It's not the boat – it's the dog,' said the father.

And peering into the sunlight Dougie could just see a hairy head and two pointed ears over the inflated red plastic side. The plaintive yapping was all but carried away by the brisk offshore wind.

'I was just giving him a ride...' sobbed the child.

'She fell and let go the string,' said her mother.

'Go and get him, Dad,' wailed one of the small boys.

'It's too deep, I've tried.'

And indeed the father was wet up to the armpits.

'You're not to go in again, Ray.' The mother was calmer than the others. She was holding her daughter's face against her sodden skirt. 'There's nothing you can do. It's not safe. We'll just have to hope for a miracle. Maybe the wind will change or something.'

The little girl lifted her head and howled again.

'Would there be a boat anywhere near?' the father asked Dougie. 'No, no boat.'

He didn't bother to say that the nearest boat was moored two miles away, and its outboard motor was lying in pieces in his own shed in Torisay.

But Dougie Bàn's eyes were shining and a look of rapture had crept over his features. He looked at the miserable child's face and knew his moment had come. He turned and ran to his van. He drove fast along the sand to the rocks at the end of the bay. As he went, his thoughts flew to St Francis, one of his favourites. He leapt across the rocks as fast as his studded working boots would allow him. Pausing for a few seconds, he watched the direction of the tiny red plastic dinghy and saw that, as he had expected, it would pass within yards of the spit of rocks at the point of the bay before being caught by the current and whisked out into the open sea.

He was down the rocks where they sloped into the water, fighting to keep his balance in the waves which washed the point. The spit was narrow, but he kept his foothold, though the eddying water prevented him from seeing where he was putting his boots. Thoughts of St Christopher passed pleasurably across his mind. Further and further he inched his way out. The dinghy came closer. The little terrier, seeing Dougie Bàn, had climbed onto the air-filled side in anticipation of rescue. It wobbled precariously.

A long string trailed behind the boat, and it seemed that as the red bubble was swept past the point the string must trail across Dougie where he stood now waist-deep awaiting it. But a contrary gust of wind struck just as the little floating balloon was at the crucial position, and whisked it sideways so that the string went trailing by just out of reach.

The little dog, seeing its rescuer receding from it, lifted its head and let out a howl of distress.

The cry for help triggered an instant response in Dougie. He threw himself forward, his hands outstretched and grabbing. His falling arm hit the string hard and dragged it down with the rest of him into the water. The jerk dislodged the dog from its slippery position, and it too was in the sea.

Like so many of the islanders, Dougie had never learned to swim. With open fingers, open mouth and open eyes he tried to climb to the surface. His head broke through once, twice, and disappeared again. The third time he came up he saw the hairy face of the little terrier paddling efficiently past him and heading for the rocks. The smile of pleasure that broke then across Dougie Bān's face was what finally sank him.

But he went down with his heart as full of joy as his lungs were full of water.

LORRAINE

1990s

When their engagement was announced, no one could believe it. Why should that bright, bonny Lorraine Wheeler want to marry a boy like that? He was as dour as a November day in Aberdeen, and about as colourless. What did she see in him? To think she could have had Jimmie Sinclair, who was two years out of law school and earning a good living already! And anyway, she'd never make a minister's wife, for goodness sake. The first time her father had seen the inside of a church was at Lorraine's wedding, and he was out again almost before the bridal couple and back behind the bar of the Craigie Arms.

From the first moment they met as students at St Andrews University Lorraine and Donald McIver had been inseparable, and when, after graduation, he had moved on to theological college Lorraine had taken a job as a secretary with a firm as close to the campus gates as she could find. They made a surprising couple even then, the plump, talkative, curly-haired Dundee girl with the energy of a puppy, and the quiet, shy, thin lad from Harris.

Even their accents were a world apart, and Donald's slowness in speech indicated his habit of thinking in Gaelic and translating into English. But he was the only person Lorraine did not interrupt in conversation.

They married a week after Donald was ordained, and if Lorraine's father felt a need at the wedding reception to drown his shame at having a minister as a son-in-law, Lorraine forgave him as a minister's wife should.

The couple's first two parishes were in the most difficult parts of inner Glasgow, and by the end of fifteen years what either of them did not know about crime, alcoholism and the lowest depths of human nature could have been inscribed on the head of a pin.

'Sodom, Gomorrah and our parish – take your pick,' laughed Lorraine, and Donald was a little shocked but knew better than to comment. Lorraine's ability to laugh at anything was matched by her sharp tongue if she felt she was being unfairly criticised. And she was not good at thinking without speaking.

It had not been Lorraine's quick tongue which had caused 'the incident', but it had certainly helped to make it worse.

Donald had started a youth club in the church hall and called it, with what he felt was pleasant ambiguity, The Three Days Club. It met three nights a week, the only evenings when he had no other events in the parish. Music featured prominently. He had managed not to object to the name chosen by the rock group which formed round two good guitarists. 'Sweet Jesus' might offend some, but Donald saw beyond it to the team spirit which he was trying to foster.

Discussion nights on any subject chosen by the members were surprisingly popular, and though he had often to modify the titles chosen for discussion, banning anything to do with sex, for example, he relished the long diatribes which gave less time for punch-ups. Smoking was allowed, though not encouraged, and as Donald pleaded with his generally critical Kirk Session, 'It is getting them in there that it is so very important. If I am too restrictive, they will not come, and how can we reach them then?'

He never said any prayers at the club, but he would shyly suggest that if anyone felt like coming to the service on Sunday, they would be made very welcome. 'What's the point?' said Lorraine. 'They'll never come.'

But she was wrong. Some did, slouching in late, sitting in the back pews with their hands in their pockets and whispering.

Donald was as happy as it was in his nature to be. He loved his wife, she loved him, their house was noisy, untidy and full of good humour punctuated by occasional flare-ups of Lorraine's impatient temper. He and the two children both knew that if they kept their heads down it would blow over quickly. Her anger seldom lasted. She was a good cook, and his meagre salary produced excellent meals.

'It's the love,' she would say when congratulated. 'It's all done with garlic, the love language of the Hebrides.'

Her jokes sometimes puzzled Donald, but he learned not to question them. He was very proud of his wife. He was also deeply proud of the club; he felt it was his only positive achievement in the parish, and one that made the daily grind of the rest worthwhile. Lorraine, meanwhile, if unorthodox in her Christianity and in her approach to parish problems, was admirable in the energy she showed as she ran various women's groups attached to the church, using her active imagination to vary the traditional fundraising activities.

'Jumble sale? How boring can you get? We'll call it "Antiques in the Making" and circularise the dealers. We need real money in this!' Her ideas did not always work, and unsold handicraft items made from eggboxes or hazelnuts piled up reproachfully in odd corners. But she kept the loyalty of the voluntary workers.

As time went on the membership of the club began to rise.

Young people were coming from the other side of Glasgow, and numbers on the music nights were becoming almost too many, Donald felt. They asked for the club to stay open till ten, and after some hesitation he allowed it. He appointed one of the older members as his stand-in for the last hour each evening, knowing his own strength was being severely tested by the long hours of parish work.

'Keep an eye on things, and just make sure there is no rowdiness,' he said. 'Let me know at once if there are any problems.'

Later they said the pathetic part had been his naivety, despite all his experience. The police raid on the Club, the seizure of drugs with the arrest and charging of several members with dealing surprised no one except Donald himself. Donald's own arrest on the doorstep of the manse and the charge of permitting illegal trading in hard drugs on premises under his control shocked the parish. The press were present, much titillated by the affair. He was released on bail pledged by the Session Clerk and returned home to a furious and distraught Lorraine at three in the morning. He was paralytically drunk. Where he had got the whisky she never discovered, but he had consumed about half a bottle which, in a man as normally abstemious as Donald, had been, to say the least, effective. He had climbed into a car which looked like his, hit two others with it, and left it parked against a tree just outside the manse.

A passing policeman, seeing the wreck, rang the manse bell on the off chance and asked innocently if the minister's wife had heard the crash or knew anything about it.

'You've a nerve, asking that!' raged Lorraine. 'It's you lot with your stupid assumptions that has driven the best man in the world to drink!'

Donald was re-arrested and this time there was no bail. The press greatly enjoyed the added dimension to the story. The subsequent court case, the fine, Donald's breakdown and departure from the parish got surprisingly little publicity nationally, happening as it did during a general election. But the local press went to town.

After Donald's slow recovery and convalescence, the Moderator of the Church of Scotland, a wise West Highlander that year, gave Donald a long interview. He convinced him that the church still needed him and that his record would not ruin his chances of another parish because there would be nothing in it except evidence of twelve years hard and devoted work in a difficult inner-city area.

'A rural parish for you, Donald, I think. You're a crofter's son, so a farming community would suit, perhaps, for the time being. There might be an opening in Dumfriesshire. No – a better idea – you're a Gaelic speaker, aren't you?'

'Not Tarbert – not on Harris,' said Donald anxiously.

'No, Torisay. Do you know it? You know about islanders, anyway. The Kirk Session of Torisay are asking for a Gaelic speaker there.'

'Do you think they will want me?' said Donald, gazing at his thumbnails.

'You can only try,' said the Moderator sympathetically.

'Of course they will want you. They'll be lucky to get you,' said Lorraine later. 'We'll go over there and see if *we* want *them*.'

Three aspiring incumbents were to preach in Torisay church on three successive Sundays, in English at the morning service and in Gaelic in the evening.

Afterwards Donald did not feel he had given of his best and Lorraine, though she didn't tell him so, thought he had flunked it by going on too long, and trying to make too many points in one sermon. But he got the job. He won because one of the other contenders flapped his wrists and was not married, and the other spoke Gaelic with an accent which made him almost completely unintelligible to the islanders, and had not gone on long enough.

'Where the hell did thon fellow learn the Gaelic?' said Danny MacLean in the Torisay Hotel bar the following night.

'The same place that he learned his English,' said Archie the Post, who knew just about everything. 'Canada. The University of Montreal.'

'Have they gone mad, that lot in Edinburgh, sending us Canada geese? What next…'

'No next. We'll be getting the Harris man.'

'Well, at least it's the same archipelago.'

After the next meeting of the Kirk Session the Session Clerk, Calum MacQueen, pinned up a notice in the church porch to say that the Reverend Donald Archibald McIver, late of the parish of Hedstoun, was to be appointed minister to the parish of Torisay as from Tuesday 17th April. Induction Service on Sunday 22nd April at 6pm, refreshments afterwards in the hall.

The first year of visits to every house on the island passed quickly for Donald. Much of his time was spent updating neglected parish records, for the last minister had been old, popular and idle about the more technical aspects of parish affairs. Donald discovered far more of what was important from Calum MacQueen than from the records.

'May Maclean hasn't been to the kirk for thirty years, but you'll have to visit, or there'll be trouble. It's not the minister she has it in for, it's the elders. They told her there was no room for her father's name with all the others on the gravestone when she had him buried. It was full up, and she'd just have to fork out for a new stone. She's that mean, she's never forgiven them, and the poor man never got his name on a stone yet.'

As in most parishes, people were divided into those who expected regular visits, and those who would do much to avoid them. Donald never found cold calling easy, and in Glasgow had learned a technique of telephoning first and saying he was coming. But here on the island not everyone had a telephone, and in any case, people considered it their right to hide in the byre or the bathroom when they saw the minister's car approaching, however far he might have trundled down a bumpy track.

He had to relearn the ways of island people; to recall it is not unfriendliness but often sheer politeness that would make someone pretend not to see you until you greeted them in case you were not in the mood for conversation that day.

'Ach, it's yourself, Reverend McIver. I was just watching the clam boats out there. And are you keeping well, now?'

He had to remind himself too that visits are long affairs, that there were many civilities to be gone through before the object of the visit might be broached; it was not good manners to press for an answer to a question or request; people liked time, maybe days, to consider things.

'Will you think about it then, Mr MacLean?'

'Yes, well. I will give it some thought. Aye.'

He remembered that, when invited to 'take your tea with us', the acceptance of 'a cup of tea in your hand' on arrival did not mean you could leave politely twenty minutes later: the main meal was still to come, with all its spread of home baking and several more cups of tea.

Once, relieving himself behind a roadside rock after one such tea, he had to pretend to be urgently bird-watching as a car went by. He told himself he must be more disciplined when accepting hospitality; but he knew he wouldn't, because he liked these old familiar ways, he liked the warm drop-scones dripping with butter, and he felt at home with the slower, more deliberate pace of life and decision-making he had known since childhood.

After a couple of years he knew he was settling into Torisay. The older people liked him because he knew the rules and they could converse comfortably with him in their first language, even though he had a Harris accent. The children liked him because he usually had sweeties in his pocket. The younger men were impressed by his ability with a football and recruited him to the island team. The crofters observed that he thought of the weather in farming terms, and not from the point of view of a tripper. The sea-going community discovered to their pleasure that he knew how to handle a lug-sail, and now he was having a boat built for him by the old boat-builder down by Baideanach in time for the island regatta in July. But even out fishing they didn't call him by his first name.

The church remained full; there had been none of the falling off a new minister expects after the first few weeks of interest, and he found this hugely encouraging. Donald would hardly have admitted he felt happy and confident, but the aching sense of failure left by his Glasgow experience was beginning to leave him.

Lorraine had more trouble in adapting to life on the island. Her natural energy and urge to start new things was frustrated. The annual round of jumble sale in April, 'Knit for your Tea' in June, Sunday School picnic in July and the church social every other month had always been up to the minister's wife to organise. But their rules and practices were inscribed in granite. Nothing, she found, could be varied in any way without causing offence.

'No, Mistress McIver, I will not be running the home baking stall this year. Having my table placed by the door in that draught last June gave me a very bad neck and the doctor says I am to take care in future.'

'But Mrs Johnstone, it's to be back in the old place, beside the teas, honest!'

'No, thank you, Mistress McIver, I have made up my mind, and there is no changing it. And how is the minister keeping?'

Lorraine got the message. She must leave established procedures alone and concentrate on new ideas, on things she knew how to do. After the doctor had mentioned he was concerned at the level of obesity on the island she decided to start aerobics classes. She consulted carefully and was encouraged by the comments.

'Yes, that would be nice.'

'Aerobics, is it? Well. We've never had that before.'

'Yes, I've seen about that on the telly.'

She put up a notice announcing a once-weekly aerobics session in the hall. The first week about a dozen children turned up, dragging fish boxes to stand on to watch through the windows. No one else came, and the next week the children didn't come either.

'You're too old,' said Neil the Pump to his wife May, 'to play aerobics, or aeroplanes or any other fancy games.; and anyway, I like you the way you are. Come on and I'll give you a squeeze...'

'I think it's disgraceful,' said Jean MacBride who seldom approved of anything done by 'these young people' whoever they might be. 'The very idea, the minister's wife prancing about in a leopard or whatever they call those swim suits.' She spat out the S's disdainfully. 'He should speak to her.'

'I think it's a shame,' said Jenny MacBride, her cousin, the school teacher. 'She really is trying, poor Lorraine. They should give her a chance. I think the doctor must have been pulling her leg, letting her think something like that would work here.'

The doctor smiled when he heard. He didn't like ministers. They upset dying people.

Donald McIver did speak to Lorraine, but mainly to thank and console her.

'Take it slowly, Lory,' he said. 'They'll take time to get used to us – you can't rush it in a place like this.'

So Lorraine sighed, and gave in, and did things as they had always been done, playing her part in the church year, running the Sunday School and wearing a hat to services. And she did her best to control her quick tongue. She made friends with Jenny MacBride, and a few others among the younger women, and they started a watercolour painting group, which nobody seemed to think was unsuitable for a minister's wife.

Though feeling underused, Lorraine was quite capable of counting her blessings. Her children loved the island and were blossoming at its excellent school, where the pupil-teacher ratio was eleven to one. The old stone manse was inconvenient but characterful and warm in winter, and the fruits of the sea and the well-hung local beef and lamb fed on the sweet herb-rich machair grazing allowed her to indulge her enjoyment of cooking. She had enough intelligent friends to stimulate and amuse her, and above all her much-loved Donald was slowly getting back to being the man she had known before everything went so unfairly wrong, and to see him content again meant everything to her.

There was only one dark cloud on the brightening McIver horizon; it was the feeling the Kirk Session was not on Donald's side. With all the tact he could muster, with patience and with understanding, he chaired the regular meetings. But he never left without the feeling that the elders were watching carefully for slips, and that after nearly two years he was still on probation.

He had no trouble with the Session Clerk, Calum MacQueen, whom he now thought of as a friend. He could consult Calum quietly, sure his words would go no further, and there were one or two others he felt happy with. But there was a faction that worried him, apparently led by Archie Lamont, the Torisay butcher, a venerable figure of some age but with needle-sharp faculties. He had been a member of the Kirk Session for thirty-five years, a figure he usually quoted when making an important statement.

Archie had a particular way of asking questions:

'You wouldn't be thinking of painting the church door a different colour from what it has been all my lifetime, I am sure, Reverend McIver.'

'Well, no, Mr Lamont, not unless others want a change.'

'Oh, that is all right, then. No change.'

On matters such as the suitability of a certain woman whom

Donald was recommending to clean the church, the butcher would look round his supporters and say gravely, 'The minister is a young man and is of course a newcomer to the island, so would not be in full possession of the facts. But I feel that as a senior member of this Kirk Session it is my bounden duty to remind members that Mrs Logan's eldest child has no known father, and I know the Session and the Presbytery would not feel happy to see the communion table or the communion silver handled by such a person.' Donald was certain the Presbytery would take no such 19th-century attitude to a respectable married woman who actually wanted the job, but the obsequious nods and mutters of agreement around the table cowed him. Most of his suggestions were met with this kind of negative reaction. He promised himself he would be more assertive as time went on, and remembered that all Kirk Sessions, drawn as they were from the most senior and sober church attenders in the community, were notoriously old-fashioned in approach. He tried to feel there was nothing personal against him in their attitude.

There was just one subject on which the Kirk Session was always in agreement, and even agreed with Donald about it – the church roof and inadequacy thereof.

'There is another damp patch in the far corner above the gallery,' said a tall, lugubrious elder from the west end of the island, a regular purveyor of bad tidings.

'Did we get an answer from the Presbytery?'

'Aye, an answer we have had,' said Calum MacQueen, 'but not the one we were looking for. We have asked for too much.'

'Well,' said Alec MacBride, 'much is what we need. If the lowest estimate is forty-five thousand to replace the roof, how can we ask for less?'

'It's the total amount they don't like,' said Donald. 'There is a fixed figure that can be passed at Presbytery level, but over that they have to go to Edinburgh for approval. And Edinburgh says it is too much to spend on one small church with a limited congregation.'

'And if we have rain pouring through on our heads, how does Edinburgh suggest that we conduct the services of a Christian community?' asked Archie Lamont coldly, his fleshy chins quivering with emotion.

'They want to know the seating capacity of the Hall.'

The timbers of the table shivered with the disapproval and disbelief that swirled around it, and now Archie Lamont got to his feet.

'The seating capacity of the Hall?' he demanded in rising tones Edith Evans could not have bettered. 'The Ha-aa—ll? Not as long as I am alive! We will fight!' he thundered, 'The people of this island have worshipped in that church since – since –'

'Since 1814,' said Donald. 'You are right, Mr Lamont. You have made a very important point.'

The butcher sat down, half-appeased, as Donald continued. 'Torisay church is beautiful, one of the finest examples of Georgian architecture in the Western Isles, and it would be a crying shame if it were to be abandoned. And we are not going to let it happen for the sake of a few thousand pounds.'

'Quite a few...' said a small shy elder, fairly newly appointed, shaking his head.

'What are we going to do, Reverend McIver then?'

The thought of taking on the power of Edinburgh was exciting and unnerving, and they all looked at the minister. The butcher cleared his throat as if he were about to speak but didn't.

'Well, first,' said Donald, 'what does the Kirk Session think of applying for the maximum grant that the Presbytery can make unilaterally and doing this at every permitted interval. We can make clear that it is only part of a major fundraising programme initiated here on the island.'

'A major programme?'

'A major fundraising programme,' repeated Donald firmly. 'I propose that we appoint a committee, and I suggest that Mrs McIver is secretary. She had a lot of fundraising experience.'

The butcher leant back and opened his mouth and shut it again. He did not approve of the minister's wife. She encouraged people to call her by her first name, for a start, and it was an outlandish name as well. Worse, she had ceased the issuing of attendance certificates in the Sunday School.

'If they don't turn up I consider it is my fault, not theirs,' she was reputed to have said. 'And in any case, the good attenders are just made to come by their mothers.'

But Archie Lamont, for all his years of experience, could not think of anyone else who would be prepared to take on fundraising for the church roof. Still, he knew he must assert himself.

'Speaking as a senior member of the Kirk Session,' he said gravely, 'it is not to my thinking that so much power should be vested in one lady, and in a matter of such importance to the community. I propose that the Session Clerk should be appointed secretary of the fundraising committee.'

There was a stir of approval.

Thank God Lorraine can't hear this, thought Donald.

'Look here,' said Calum MacQueen, 'we are coming up to haying, and I have quite enough to do on the croft and with the Session minutes without being secretary to any committees. I don't mind being the treasurer if you want. And I don't see what's wrong with the minister's wife.'

Archie Lamont glared at the elders, clearly daring anyone else to challenge his authority.

'Well,' said the minister mildly, 'will someone else volunteer to be secretary, or suggest a name, perhaps? Whoever it is would report to the Kirk Session, of course.'

The elders all looked down at the table. After a pause the butcher spoke again.

'It is quite clear that the fundraising should be ordered by the proper authority, which is the Kirk Session itself.'

His gaze passed round the table and just missed Alec MacBride raising his eyes heavenward. Two other elders exchanged glances.

'Well, may I suggest,' said the minister, 'that we put it to a vote. We need a fundraising committee, and the committee needs leadership, and Mrs McIver is the only volunteer we have. The alternative is that the Kirk Session takes on the whole project, as Mr Lamont suggests.'

'Never in the history of this Kirk Session, and I have been a member for nigh on thirty-six years, never has any matter been decided by a *vote*.' The butcher said the word as if it had a dirty connotation. 'Here in Torisay, Reverend McIver, we always make decisions by agreement.'

Donald was amazed at his own courage. 'But if we have no agreement, Mr Lamont, surely the sensible thing is to see how many are in favour of either proposal, and agree to go with the majority? Isn't that fair?'

The butcher was speechless. Before he could pull himself together Calum MacQueen spoke.

'See here, I'll give you each a bit of paper, and you can write your vote on it, fold it up and pass it to me. It's a secret ballot, and that's an end to it.'

'Aye,' said a voice down the table, 'That will do, and then we can get away. It's late, so it is.'

'And whatever is decided, I'll be treasurer,' Calum added.

The votes were counted at eight to one in favour of the minister's wife. So, in silence, Archie Lamont acquiesced, and the minister's motion was passed.

'The butcher looked as if he has swallowed the dish cloth,' said Neil MacNeill to his wife over a cup of tea later.

'That man's trouble,' she replied tersely.

Meanwhile the minister gave his wife an edited version of the meeting, saying that after discussion she had been chosen for the job.

Donald and Lorraine both threw themselves with enthusiasm into the fundraising. Lorraine was more than pleased to have something at last to absorb her energy.

'I'll give them something to think about,' she said. 'I'll stir this place up.'

'Careful, dear…'

'Don't call me dear, Donald McIver – it's so patronising. Jenny MacBride at the school, we'll get her on the committee. And Catriona Wise – she's a ball of fire. We'll really get this going.'

There was no holding her. Donald McIver had to justify her expenses again and again, but as the elders saw the money coming in they became less reluctant to spend. Publicity was the first thing: late at night Lorraine and Jenny worked away at the school computer. After initial hesitation every islander was paying for and displaying a 'SAVE TORISAY CHURCH' poster in their front window, except for the butcher, who never put any poster in his window except one saying 'Jesus saves', and never would.

'Well, that's all right,' cracked Archie the Post. 'We need all the saving help we can get, so we do. Anyway, Mona Lamont says she's not paying good money for a poster just to throw it away, and she's got it up in the back window of the butcher's van. There'll be a fair humdinger if he takes it down, just you see…'

Then came the programme Lorraine's committee called privately MTT, for Milk the Trippers. The school-children collected sacksful of dark carragheen weed from the rocks at the low spring tide. This was handed to the Women's Wednesday Group, normally occupied with unravelling old sweaters and re-knitting them for the Red Cross. Now they spent their evenings washing and sorting the weed, drying it in the sun, and packing tiny quantities into little plastic bags and sticking on persuasive labels devised by Jenny:

Carragheen Weed,
the traditional medicine of the Hebrides,
gathered from pure Atlantic waters.
The Green way to Health

Stewed gently in milk, the resulting jelly can be applied internally
or externally. Taken regularly it is reputed to relieve many ailments,
including rheumatism, lumbago, arthritis, tennis elbow and other
conditions.
Smoothed gently into the skin at night it is said to
preserve youthful appearance and vitality.

SOLD IN AID OF THE SAVE TORISAY CHURCH FUND

'Jenny,' said Lorraine, laughing, 'you are such a fraud! Rheumatism, maybe, but all the rest? And skin cream?'

'It'll do them no harm,' said Jenny. 'I have been very careful about the Trade Descriptions Act, you'll notice.'

The tourists loved it, and bought it, and all the other things displayed on the stall down by the pier.

'People can't resist buying something to take home after a visit to a new place,' said Lorraine. 'And they'll get something more interesting than souvenir mugs here.'

Bags of cooked winkles, pins included, could be bought to eat on the ferry on the way back to the mainland. Freshly baked scones, rock buns, oatcakes, and crumpets all sold fast, and there was never enough freshly made butter, stamped with moulds of thistles or shells, to satisfy the demand. Green rush baskets full of mushrooms were popular, and bunches of wild watercress, especially with the day trippers.

The painting group worked furiously. There was some talent there and watercolours of beaches and hills, sheep and blackhouses sold well, more evocative in their transparent colours of the vivid turquoise and deep purples of the sea over the white shell sand than the postcards in the Torisay store. The Kirk Session had baulked initially at the purchase of cardboard mounts for the pictures, but had to admit that they were paying off. A gallery in Oban expressed interest.

'So now,' crowed Jenny, after conducting negotiations, 'we're exporting as well!'

Catriona Wise, the vet's wife, ran the stall and was endlessly imaginative in guessing what the tourists might buy. Smooth mottled stones, or stones with holes in them seemed to appeal. The plain stones striped and banded with quartz veins which lay all over the beaches of the Atlantic shore suddenly became desirable when labelled 'Celtic doorstop', or 'Hebridean paperweight', and were bought. Small pebbles of agate and purple jasper, red carnelian and blue flint, and especially the little eggs of pink and white quartz were snapped up once they had spent some time in the stone polisher which someone had dug out of a cupboard. Catriona checked their names in 'Pebbles on the Beach' from the school library.

Shell earrings, oddly shaped stones with eyes of birds or seals, limpet shell hats stuck on stone faces – the small things went well, especially to children.

Archie MacPhail from Brodach watched in astonishment a group of trippers picking and choosing the different colours from Catriona's carefully labelled bowls of pebbles. When they had finished, he stepped forward and stroked a large, many-facetted stone of speckled granite marked 'A centrepiece for the Rockery, £4.99'.

'Good heavens,' he said, his eyes unfocused and misty with speculation. 'Go-ooo-ood heavens. That beach in front of my house must be worth millions...'

'Well, you and Mairi get down there and bring me some good stones,' said Catriona sharply. 'It's the marketing that matters.

They're worth nothing lying there looking at you, and I haven't the time, I'm that busy here…'

'They asked for bread and you gave them a stone…' said Archie, still far away.

'They can get their bread here too, if they want it. And just tell Mairi we could do with some more of her oatcakes. I'm putting up the price, they go so well. "Mairi's Special Recipe" we're calling them.'

Someone else was keeping a close eye on the stall. From the window of his shop Archie Lamont watched enviously the small crowd of trippers who always clustered round the long wooden table when the ferry was in, trippers who might have been persuaded, perhaps, to buy his home-made haggis and black pudding, which had sold much better before folk were tempted by the rubbish the minister's wife was purveying. He could hardly complain, though, as the Church Roof Fund was certainly growing. He still smarted over the defeat he had suffered about the voting, which he was sure the islanders would know about, and the success of that woman's fundraising added to the insult. If only he could catch her trying to trade on a Sunday he would reassert his damaged authority. Or doing something illegal, perhaps. Revenge would be sweet.

Lorraine's latest idea was to gather sheep's wool where it lay sticking to clumps of heather, or caught on the fence wires. She had it washed and bagged up, and it sold steadily. *Undyed traditional island wool, from free-range blackface-cross sheep, washed and prepared for spinning or stuffing cushions.*

'What about "happy, laughing sheep" while you're about it?' said Donald, smiling at Lorraine as she stuck the labels on the bags late one evening.

She smiled down at her work. To hear him making jokes again was so good. He was relaxed now, like his old self. Having helped to organise something with real potential had done him so much good, restoring his confidence in himself. That rot in the church roof is the best thing that could have happened to us, thought his wife.

'I'm wondering about a shellfish stall next summer, too. Mussels, cockles. If we could persuade the lobster men each to give us one lobster a week, and some of those brown crabs that they just throw back – they'd sell like anything, and at a price. Knitted goods too, next summer. We'll get the knitters to keep going during the winter months, so we have lots of stock. The tourists will stop coming soon, well, from September, when the weather won't be so good. Can we do any more begging letters? Did you get an answer from the architectural group, Donnie?'

'Yes – five hundred pounds. Not bad. But I'm hoping for a lot more from the Scottish Tourist Board. Those photographs of the church seem to have impressed them, and I told them about the donations we are getting in the porch box now the trippers know the church is in danger. Do you know, Lory, by Wednesday we will have eleven thousand pounds in the campaign account, and we've only been going four months?'

'And I think the second auction will bring in even more than the first one. I'm going to make sure those Glasgow dealers know about the old things people are bringing out of their lofts. And after that we'll do fifty per cent for the church, and fifty for the donors, and that will bring out more still. We're on our way, Donnie boy!'

He picked a sticker out of the box and laid it across his wife's forehead.

I HELPED SAVE TORISAY CHURCH, it read. Hardly a tripper left the island without buying one for his backpack or car window.

'Awa an' play yersel, wee Donnie,' she said. 'Ah'm buzzy.'

The fund continued to grow, that winter and during the next summer. As time went by the initial interest wavered, some islanders feeling they had done enough and going back to their own business. But the hard core remained, and the committee agreed in August that another eighteen months should do it, and reported to the Session Clerk.

'Well,' he said, 'the roof's not mending itself. There'll be more slates gone before the New Year, and there's not a lot to hold the rest on.'

'Calum,' said the minister, 'I'll get that roof replaced if it's the last thing I do.'

Calum remembered his words later.

A pair of trippers came in one day at the end of August, stayed one night, and went away on the ferry next day, munching on Catriona's potato scones as they leant over the rail watching the hill tops of the island sink into the western sunset.

'I'm sure that was the name. I'm sure it was. What a funny place to find him.'

He repeated this unthinkingly to a friend he met who was a stringer for a Glasgow newspaper, who repeated it to his contact, who brought it up at the *Scottish Morning* weekly editorial conference. Being August, they were short of news, so they decided to send someone over to see if there was a story.

The first reporter, given the instructions, said he got seasick, and it was his aunt's funeral anyway.

'Send Andrews. He loved the sea.'

Tom Andrews hated the sea and anything to do with it, but he knew he was past his best and on his way out in his editor's eyes, so couldn't afford to say no.

'A colour piece, that's what we want,' said the Features Editor. 'A life rebuilt in the peace of the Outer Isles – get some pics of the island, and of him – McIver. Read up the story. About three years ago. Nice scandal.'

It was a day of low cloud and grey drizzle, and though the crossing was not unduly rough Andrews was endlessly sick on the boat. The *Morning* photographer with him got some pleasure out of raising his camera each time his companion vomited, for which Andrews hit him on the side of the face. They both arrived in Torisay angry and fed up with the assignment. They asked for the Reverend Donald McIver in the Torisay store, and had no trouble in finding the manse, which was set behind a low stone wall just outside the village. They were very obviously strangers in their puffed anoraks and town shoes, and even without the outsize camera they were seen as no ordinary trippers.

'It'll be more of them twitchers,' said Davy Bell, watching from the door of the hotel.

'We had two of them stuck in the bog behind our place,' said Archie MacPhail. 'I thought I'd need the tractor to get them out, but my wee dog went in with a rope for them. What a sight!'

'What will they be wanting with the minister, then? They're away off to the manse.'

'Maybe they're no twitchers after all. Maybe they're from the Department about the church.'

'Aye,' said Davy, 'that'll be it. Hey, Lachy John, come over here.'

The postmaster's son was sitting on a box, listening.

'Just take a walk up past the manse, Lachy John, and see what's going on.'

'OK, Davy – do I get some crisps?'

'Aya, take some crisps, son. They're on the bar.'

The boy ran off up the hill and as he came near the manse sauntered along eating out of his crisp packet and idly kicking a stone, which took him from one side of the road to the other.

Lorraine had seen the two men from her front window and knew at once what they were. She had met their kind before.

She was at the door before they were.

'Good afternoon,' said Andrews, panting slightly.

Lorraine did not reply.

'Is this where the Reverend Donald McIver lives?'

'It may be,' said Lorraine coldly.

'Is he at home?'

'Why do you want him?'

'I would like to have a few words with him. Is he here?'

'Who – are – you?' She enunciated the words separately and icily. The photographer tittered.

'I am Tom Andrews of the *Scottish Morning*, and I have been asked by my editor to get an interview with Mr McIver, late of Hedstoun in Glasgow.'

'You – have – been – what?' Electric currents seemed to be emanating from Lorraine's rigid body. Her hand gripped the door-jam and her eyes bored into the journalist.

He hesitated, and the photographer giggled again.

Andrews looked at his notebook.

'Are you Mrs Lorraine McIver, wife of a minister called Donald McIver who ran the Hedstoun Youth Club in Glasgow when…'

'Get – out!' The venom in her voice shook him. Only the irksome presence of the photographer kept him going.

'May I speak to the Reverend McIver, please?'

'May – you – nothing. May you be forgiven for coming to this place at all.' Her voice was rising. 'It was you filthy people with your filthy speculation that as near as … as near as … nearly killed a good man. And did you care? And now you've found him and you're after him again! You filthy, slimy ratpack, you!'

She took a step towards Andrews, brandishing her fist, her eyes wild. The photographer had already backed away at the verbal onslaught, on the pretext of taking a photograph of this startling woman.

'Get out of my house! Get out of my garden! Get off this island and don't you ever show your filthy noses here again!'

Andrews tried to stand his ground, but the sheer vehemence of the woman made him step back into a saucer of cat's milk which skidded away from him across the wet doorstep as he fell the other way. His elbow hit the corner of the step. He rolled over onto his knees and climbed to his feet as the door slammed with a sound that, as Davy Bell said later, must have been heard at the west end.

The photographer was laughing helplessly against the garden wall, and anger rose in Andrews like boiling milk in a pan. He clutched his agonising elbow.

'You fucking idiot,' he snarled, 'Did you get that? Where's your fucking camera? Did you get her hitting me? I'll have the bitch for assault. She's broken my arm.'

The photographer was creasing himself with delight.

'She never hit you, Tom. She's half your size, and you ran! And you've broken her saucer – *she'll* have *you*! Aw, Tom, wait till the boys hear this one!'

By the time Andrews had been to the doctor's surgery and been asked if he had ever heard of a 'funny bone', the boat had left for the mainland. The two journalists checked into the hotel, to Davy Bell's delight. Lachy John's breathless description of the Battle of the manse had been riveting but inadequate.

'She was that pink in the face, and the big man had milk all over his trousers. No, I didn't hear what he said, but he was in a fair way about it, so I just ran.'

In the hotel bar that night Andrews glowered into his empty whisky glass. Silence had fallen as he walked in, and he knew they had been talking about him, and probably laughing, too, at his rout by the minister's wife. He had had another row with the photographer, and they were no longer on speaking terms. His anger and resentment at the humiliation by the woman was gnawing at his belly.

He had tried to engage some of the men who stood round the bar in conversation, but had not got far. Straight questions, such as, 'How long has your minister been here?' met with evasive answers.

'Well, I wouldn't rightly know, not being from Torisay myself. I live up on the north side.'

Other questions appeared to be wilfully misunderstood.

'His wife's a bit of a harridan, isn't she?'

'No, Mistress McIver is from the mainland, Dundee, they say, on the east coast.'

'What do you think of her?'

'Well, now, if you were thinking of giving money for Torisay church, that's the lady for you. She runs the campaign.'

Andrews persisted. 'Where does *he* come from, McIver, do you know?'

'He comes from where all good ministers come – from the theological college.'

Laughter from the listening drinkers. They were making fun of him. He tried buying drinks, which were accepted but did not open any mouths, except one – a small man who wanted to tell him a long story about the iniquity of the Crofters Commission.

Eventually, angry and frustrated, his second whisky working in him, Andrews interrupted his companion.

'Listen, you. Listen all of you. I'm going to tell you all something. Did you know your blessed minister was convicted of running a drugs club in Glasgow? Of selling smack to kids? Did you know he was convicted of drunken driving? Stealing a car? Did you know that?'

At last he had the attention of the entire bar. The muttering started as his words were repeated in English and in Gaelic. He looked round and knew he had hit the bullseye which would get him what he wanted. They – didn't – know! Now he had his angle.

He ordered another double. Then pulling his notebook out of his pocket with the tourist leaflet he had from the ferry, he planned his revenge.

Meanwhile, up the hill, in front of the manse fire, Donald sat in his armchair. Lorraine was sitting on the floor, her head against his knee.

'I don't really know, Donnie. But I could just *feel* they were bad… No, I wasn't rude, really, just angry. They have no business here… Well, maybe I was a wee bit rude, but he went on and on. He was on about Hedstoun – that was it. The nerve!'

'You shouldn't have spoken with them, Lory. I would have dealt with it when I came in. It may be about the church campaign, you know? What paper did you say?'

'I know, like they told us last time. I should just have said "No comment". But I wasn't ready for it, Donnie.'

He put his hand up to his head and rubbed his eyes wearily.

'Donnie, will you promise me something?'

'What's that?' he said.

'Promise?'

'Yes. What?'

'If they come back, and I don't think they will, but if they do; if they ask you about Hedstoun and all that. Promise – you'll say "No comment," just like they told us. "No comment."'

'You're right, Lory. No, I promise. But dearie, it could be something quite different.'

It was not yet dark when Andrews left the bar, which led him to think it was earlier than it was. He was only slightly drunk, but in no state to worry about relative sunset hours at different latitudes. The photographer had disappeared, so he arrived at the manse alone at 9pm.

Donald answered the door. At this time of night it was usually a parishioner in some kind of trouble.

Andrews blurted out his question with only a rushed preamble.

'Tom Andrews, *Scottish Morning*, my editor wants me to ask you, McIver, if you think it was right and hon – honable – honourable to hide the scandal of your convictions in Glasgow from the people – these people who employed you here?'

Donald was flabbergasted.

'I – I – you…'

'Donald!' A sharp voice from behind him. Andrews recognised it.

'Go on,' he snarled, 'They don't know, do they? You never told them!'

'Donald!'

'No comment,' said Donald, his voice shaking. A hand came past him and closed the door.

Tom Andrews, chuckling happily, stumbled down the hill towards the call box. He fumbled in his pocket for his charge card and the copy he had already written at the bar.

'No, Jock,' he said when he got through. 'I don't want Features – I want the News desk.'

He had never felt more sober.

It is possible that if the News Editor had been in the office that night, rather than at his daughter's birthday party, the story might not have been used the next morning in the form that it was phoned in. But the Deputy News Editor was longing to go home, and the third page was weak even for August, so he passed it straight on to the subs. It was the right length, so they left it alone.

It is possible, too, though unlikely, that if the butcher had not looked down as he wrapped Nan MacFarlane's Sunday roast three days later he would not have seen the article.

He produced it at the Kirk Session meeting the following evening. He asked the minister to leave the hall so that the meeting could go into Special Session.

Donald said, 'I would like to stay. I believe you will give me the chance to defend myself, though I do not deny the essence of the article.'

Before anyone else could reply, Archie Lamont said coldly, 'The Kirk Session has the right to request your absence while it discusses matters concerning your employment, Mr McIver.'

With the minister gone, he read aloud extracts from the article. Although most of those present had seen it, no one else was prepared to raise the matter.

DRINK–DRUGS MINISTER'S HEBRIDEAN HIDEOUT.

The Rev. Donald McIver (41), convicted of drink-driving and car theft offences while under investigation by the Drugs Squad, has managed to put it all behind him. How? Because no one knows who he is! Living comfortably in his stone-built Victorian mansion on a holiday paradise island, whose dazzling white shell-sand beaches are washed by the Gulf Stream, he has no regrets...'

In the picturesque old-world village of Torisay, with a tiny congregation drawn from a population of a mere 650, McIver has landed on his feet. His old parishioners in the slums of Glasgow would not know him, disguised by a beard and living off the fat of the land. His wife Lorraine (39), sees herself as running the island, chairing local committees and abusing those who fail to meet with her approval.

... His unsuspecting congregation were appalled to discover that the man they trusted as their pastor has a past that reads like a lurid paperback...

... McIver refused last night to justify or comment on his failure to reveal to the people of Torisay his past involvement in drink and drugs...

What the Church of Scotland must ask itself:

Should a Christian community be led by one who has succumbed to alcoholism?

Should a man who has misled children by running a club where drugs were freely available be in moral charge of young people?

Was the Church right to conceal these facts from a community innocently seeking a new pastor?

Scottish Morning *says NO – NO – NO! The Church has let these people down!*

Archie Lamont could not have put it better himself, but he tried. It was a full meeting, and there was little argument over the Kirk Session table.

'I ask you,' thundered the butcher, in his most John Knoxian mode, 'I ask you here in the sight of the Lord, can you find it in your Christian consciences to allow this man, this man with all his deviousness and hypocrisy, with his sins weighing like millstones round his neck, to stay in this community of good people whose trust he has so grievously abused?'

'Och, come on, Archie, you're not going to drive the poor man out without even giving…' tried the Session Clerk.

'Without what, Calum MacQueen? Do you believe that he will deny that of which he stands accused? He has been put to the test, and he has been found wanting.'

In the end, with more protest from Calum, supported nervously by Neil MacNeill and one or two others, the butcher declared this was for once the occasion for a vote. The motion was that a letter be drafted to the Presbytery asking that they set in motion the procedures for the removal and replacement of the Torisay minister. It was passed by a majority of six to four, with two abstentions.

That was almost the end of it, as far as the island was concerned. Of course there was anger from some islanders, but the 'they can't do this' and the 'it's a terrible shame' factions were in the minority, and had no influence on the Kirk Session anyway.

'What about the campaign?' asked one elder.

'The campaign will go on, and in a more dignified and respectable way than hitherto,' Archie Lamont said portentously. 'I will run it myself.'

And the campaign did go on, with money trickling in from

tourist donations and the occasional jumble sale. But Lorraine's friends would have no more to do with it. The life went out of it, and the slates continued to slide off the church roof.

After the departure of the McIvers, on a painfully beautiful late September day, the life of the island went on, not much changed. The congregation of Torisay church endured a long winter of visiting theological students preaching in the church with no Gaelic but plenty of visual aids.

'You know what this one had in his pocket? A string of wee flags! Bunting! All colours! "Do you know what this is?" he said. What age does he think we are?'

But the following spring they got a new minister, a native of Mull, and near retirement. He was not worried about holding services in the church hall.

Lorraine took the broken Donald back to Dundee, to her father's house. Her father was retired now, having sold his two pubs to a brewery. She eased Donald through the winter, taking him regularly to the clinic and watching his depression very slowly come under control. He was so wrapped up in himself that he hardly noticed Lorraine was seeing a lot of Jimmie Sinclair again, now a Writer to the Signet with big offices in Edinburgh.

It was eighteen months before this affair came to a conclusion. The day came when Lorraine took Donald for a long walk out in the country, and sitting on a hill top looking out towards the North Sea she broke the news to him.

'Donnie, it's all over,' she said.

'Over, Lory?' said Donald, 'What do you mean, over?'

'It's finished, Donald. They've settled. Two hundred and fifty thousand pounds in an out-of-court settlement, and it's all ours – tax free! And an apology, next Monday, in *my* words, on the same page of the f...ing *Scottish Morning*.' She used a very unladylike word which made Donald blink. 'Ooh, and do I love to think of the costs they'll have to pay too! Don't leave your mouth open, wee Donnie – you'll catch a fly. Listen – I'll tell you all about it.'

'Lory, you are amazing,' said Donald. 'What have you done? I don't know how I'll ever…'

'Don't thank me,' said Lorraine, 'thank Jimmie Sinclair. And thank my Dad – he put the money up front, and he knew he could have lost it all. And thank Jenny MacBride. She has kept me going through all this with her letters, and it was Jenny that first pointed out that the words "his past involvement with drink and drugs" could actually be libellous. That's when I got in touch with Jimmie. Jenny is the one who most deserves our thanks.'

'Jenny MacBride! Well, well…' said Donald. 'What you two get up to… Well, I know how we will thank *her*. We don't need all that money.'

Lorraine made a face, though she had known how it would be, and she loved Donald the way he was.

And that is how Torisay church got its new roof, and its new windows, and a new coat of paint inside (which caused a great deal of argument over the colour) and a new lease of life.

Lorraine started a very successful co-operative mail order service for home-knitted woollens. Donald became Classics master at an independent school in Perthshire, also teaching Gaelic as a special subject. But very few of the boys and girls opted to learn it.

IAN

2000s

The big man stood in the light of the early morning watching two small boys fishing in the harbour from the height of the dark, waterlogged wooden edge of the pier. They swung their weighted lines round their heads, like cowboys throwing lariats, and hurled them far out into the water. The hooks were baited with the torn flesh which spilled like half-cooked egg yolk from the smashed blue mussel shells scattered at their feet. The lead weights dropped through the oily surface with a dull plonk to be dragged in hand over hand, trailing the bait over the heads of the apathetic fish which scoured the harbour mud. Occasionally a flapping silvery tiddler would be pulled in to be eagerly examined and discussed and then flung high and back into the water. Usually a herring gull would scoop it up before it had time to recover from its flight. What was the point? the big man thought. Fishing for fishing's sake...

He turned away from this unpromising sport to where the ferry boat was being loaded. His car had been on board for an hour already, and he was irritated by the delay, since he had timed his arrival in the little west coast town to coincide with the boat's scheduled departure time. It was now becoming clear that the departure was indefinitely postponed.

The reason for this was a bull, a large brown bull with white legs and a white head which had so far successfully resisted all attempts to persuade it to leave the mainland and venture onto the high seas. It had been pushed, pulled, poked, kicked, shouted at, blindfolded, cajoled and tempted with handfuls of grass from the back of the bus shelter, but nothing would induce it to set more than one tentative foot on the metal ramp which led onto the boat. It was resting, now, tied by its halter rope to the side of the crate in which it had travelled by lorry to this point. It stood with its head slightly drooping and its eyes half-shut, looking singularly content.

The second mate was arguing with the lorry driver.

'Just why,' he said, in exasperated tones, 'can you not give us the loan of it for the two days? On Saturday morning I'll have it back here on the pier, there's no doubt about that.'

'Because in two days I'll be down in Sussex and there'll be another beast in thon crate.'

'You've surely got other crates, with all them bulls?'

'That's no' my business.' The driver folded his arms. 'If I went back without the crate the boss would have me for his tea.'

'Here,' said the second mate, very conciliatory, 'here's what we'll do. We'll go along to the pier master's office and we'll get on the telephone to your boss, and explain the situation.'

'He'll no be in till half eight, maybe later,' the driver smirked.

The second mate sent a message to the captain, who sent one back to the effect that he was willing to wait another hour and a half. It would mean missing the tide at the first island on his run, but he could take it in on the way back the following day. At this point the big man, who saw his own convenience affected by this change of plan, decided to step in.

'Excuse me, but can't you leave the bull here and collect it on another trip when there is a crate available?'

'And where would we leave it?' said the second mate sarcastically. 'In the pier master's office?'

He swung round to face this new irritation, but instead of speaking again his mouth stayed open as he looked up at the big man in the belted raincoat. Then he turned away and his eyes became unfocused as he stared into the distance, trying to remember. The voice had a slight transatlantic twang, but there was something familiar in those narrow lips and cold eyes. If there had been less flesh about the face, he could have sworn...

The lorry driver meanwhile had walked away to his cab, where he was rummaging in the pocket of a jacket.

'Just a moment,' said the big man. 'Leave this to me. I think I can fix it.'

He walked over to the driver and touched his elbow.

'Here, have one of mine.' He put his expensive-looking lighter back in his pocket. 'There has to be a way round this. How much are those crates worth?'

The driver looked at the glowing end of the cigarette he held between finger and thumb, then looked sideways at the big man and named a figure they both knew to be at least double the value of the crate. They agreed after a short discussion on about one and a half times with one third to be paid in cash.

'Done,' said the big man. 'Now you get that bull back in the crate.'

The bull was in the crate within seconds of the driver producing a capful of food nuts from his cab ('We could have done with that stuff an hour ago,' said the second mate bitterly) and in no time the crate, bull and all, was swinging through the air and down onto the car desk of the ferry.

As the boat moved out of the harbour the big man went into the small cafeteria on the main deck and carried a cup of tea to a table.

'You always think you can buy your way out of trouble. You think money solves everything.'

That was the sort of thing she said when he had dealt with a problem, and he could see now the way her features sharpened when she was attacking him, her lips tightening, her eyes narrowing. He never understood the attitude, but he remembered the loathing in her look.

He lifted the cup to his lips and after a sip set it down again on the saucer. It tasted of nothing resembling tea, so why drink it? He ate his bacon roll, and then fought with the clear wrapping of a small packet of biscuits, which broke as they fell on the table. It was so typical of this country, he thought. They couldn't even wrap biscuits so you could open them without a pair of scissors. Nothing had changed, except for the worse. He remembered when breakfast on the ferry had been a bowl of good porridge and a kipper, a real kipper with a backbone which peeled away from the succulent flesh. Not that he could have paid for the breakfast in those days. It had been a jelly piece and cheese brought from home, then. Now that he could afford the breakfast, he couldn't get it.

It would be another two hours before they got in, so he walked up on the deck and stood with the wind in his face looking out towards his destination. Strangely, he felt no particular emotion about this journey. He had thought he might.

The boat was much bigger and none of the crew members was known to him, though some were probably from the island. Otherwise the crossing was exactly as he remembered it: the outlines of coast and islands; the solitary sentinel figures of the lighthouses; the heaving grey coldness of the waves; even the screaming herring gulls wheeling endlessly over the white stream

of the wake, scanning it for floating garbage, keeping up effort-
lessly with the boat like satellites surrounding a planet, ten times
great-grandchildren of the gulls which had followed that other
ferry going in the opposite direction – even the gulls were iden-
tical. It was as though nothing had noticed he had been away.
It felt unreal, as if he were not taking part in the journey but
watching it on film happening to someone else.

On that last ferry trip, going the other way, there had been
no lack of emotion. There had been anger. There had been frus-
tration. He had stood at the rail, as he did now, but clenching
it with whitened knuckles, with his face turned towards the
mainland, determinedly not looking back and concentrating
only on not allowing one drop of the ocean of resentment inside
him to trickle from his burning eyes. He knew as a fact that was
how it had been but he could not remember how it had felt. He
just remembered that the boat journey had been bad. Afterwards
too much had happened for there to be time for any regrets.

When the island had been in sight for half an hour, other
passengers, day trippers and islanders, began to gather at the
rail. It was a grey day, and windy, but the clouds were high and
there were patches of blue sky appearing and disappearing in the
north-west. The big man was aware of people around him and he
avoided catching anyone's eye. One older woman in particular
stared at him curiously. He did not recognise her and pretended
not to notice.

The boat edged into the pier, ropes were flung, shouts
exchanged. The second mate, supervising the raising of the pas-
senger gangway from below, looked along the rail and nudged
the deckhand beside him.

'Yon big fellow in the mack. That's Ian Macrae. John Archie's
boy.'

The pier was more crowded, busier than Ian remembered it.
Twenty or more cars were drawn up behind the storage shed,

either meeting the boat or joining it. He walked down the gangway and then stood aside while his car was driven over the ramp from the car deck. He climbed in quickly and steered it through the gateway onto the track. No, it was more than a track now. It was paved, and there was a small car park.

He drove slowly over the stone bridge and through Torisay, which was still not much more than a scattering of houses growing out of the green of the machair a little way from the harbour. He paused briefly to buy some cigarettes. Where the little shop had been there was now a flourishing general store, selling food, hardware, postcards, sweets and the small objects tourists have to buy to show they have set foot in a place. The rest seemed much the same. The butcher's shop and the stone-fronted hotel looked as he remembered; the sheep still grazed from one side of the road to the other and the hens still scratched round the houses. It was too familiar, still, after all these years, to look at objectively as a stranger might. He felt an uncomfortable distaste for it all, as when opening a long-shut drawer and seeing old, recognised, forgotten possessions which are no longer relevant. He felt the same urge to forget it all again.

After a mile the unfenced road began to rise and fall and weave its way among clusters of rock at the foot of the hill which dominated this part of the island. It was not very high, nor very steep, but all man-made objects, roads, buildings, fences and walls took their positions and directions from the dictates of its rolling flanks. This was something he had thought about when he was far away and saw how the routes of motorways and pylons slashed through natural lines, carving up the countryside like dead meat. But once he was into road building he had seen the economics of the direct approach.

The coastline swung closer and further, never long out of sight. Small bays fringed with pale shell sand were strung along the shore behind mounds and cliffs of sand dunes, separated by long straggles of barnacled rock. He thought of rubber boots slipping, splashing into small rock pools, onto pink coral lining dotted with jelly-red sea anemones.

The sky was clearing now over the island, and the shadow of the fast-moving cloud layer was drawn away like a veil to the north-east, exposing water and shore to a brilliant sunlight.

Pausing on a rise, Ian pulled his car into a passing place. He sat watching the waves as they swept layer upon layer into one of the wider beaches, breaking and withdrawing, giving and taking in their endless love affair with the shore. In the Bahamas, he thought, the sand was white like this, the shallow water this same shocking turquoise green, giving way to the rich purple-blue of the deeper sea.

He got out and leaned against the bonnet, lifting his collar against the sharp wind while the dazzling sunlight in his eyes had him reaching mentally for the sunglasses he had not brought with him. It was this wind that kept those beaches the way they were: anywhere else in the world they would have been covered with oily tans under multi-coloured sun shades, the water full of screaming bodies plunging and playing in the surf. Stone cabins on the dunes would have been dispensing spiced barbecued meat on skewers and that disgusting mango-flavoured ice cream which had always been her favourite. He shook his head and shook the scenes from his mind. Here only the gulls screamed on the beach, while little scurrying groups of ringed plovers fussily scoured the water's edge for anything interesting the waves might have left on the wet sand.

The springy machair turf felt familiar under his polished brown shoes which looked strangely at odds with their surroundings. A little patch of eyebright winked up at him, and he frowned back at the tiny flower. He had forgotten its name. 'Nature study' as his teacher, Miss Louden, had called it, was not one of his favourite subjects as a small boy, and when it became 'biology' it had frankly bored him.

The impatient malaise that had been with him for the last few days was leaving him now, and he felt a sudden reluctance to arrive. Nervous, even. He knew what he had come for, but it didn't seem quite so simple now he was nearly there. He lit a cigarette, dropping the film wrapping from the new packet.

Through half-closed eyes he watched the languid progress of a grey heron over the bay and then decided there was no point in wasting more time. He turned back to the car. He straightened his tie in front of the window that reflected the sky behind him and smoothed his ruffled hair. They would see the difference, he thought, as the wind lifted again the layer he always drew over the thinning patch on the crown of his head.

At the thought of his parents, he loosened his tie and pulled it off, throwing it onto the back seat. He did not want to look imposing. It was vital that the atmosphere should be easy from the start. Everything depended on it.

He drove on to where he could see the small township of Balinbeag spread round the convex curve of the low hill, a scattered handful of white-painted stone houses randomly placed on the machair, all end-on to the prevailing wind as it swept in from the sea. There was one large building which had not been there before, and football posts nearby showed it to be a new school.

The scene framed by his windscreen would have appeared to a stranger like a picture postcard of Highland peacefulness. But Ian saw it as he knew it, a real place, a place of forgotten passions, remembered boredom and other conflicting emotions which had ultimately driven him away.

His parents' croft house stood a little back from the others, facing the drained marshland which ran back across the island from the bay. There was more fencing than he remembered, but the grazing sheep looked as if they had not moved since he had last seen them.

He felt prepared, now, for the dramatic moment of the knock, the opening door, the meeting and greeting on the doorstep of his old home.

But it was not quite like that. There was no answer when he knocked on the front door, and after a few moments he walked round the back of the house. He noticed the sparkling white of new Snowcem on the walls. His father must be keeping fit then, maintaining his habit of repainting every other year.

As he turned the corner, he took in a new shed which stood by the remains of the old one, the pile of metal-framed lobster creels, and then, with a shock, his mother. She was standing with her back to him, one hand on her hip, a bucket in the other, watching the hens pecking on the worn ground for the scattered mixture of cooked potato peelings and corn. He had been unprepared for her almost totally grey hair. She was smaller, her neck and head emerged from her shoulders at a lower angle and her face, he noticed as she turned, was more lined. But as she saw him and threw her head back the lines seemed to disappear as the skin tautened, her eyes widened and her mouth fell slightly open.

After the barest pause, she said, 'Ian.' It was a statement, made quietly to herself, not a greeting.

'Hullo, Mother.'

'Come away in.' She walked past him still carrying the bucket, not meeting his eye. She would never have wanted any display of emotion out of doors, where the neighbours might see, he thought. He followed her, ducking his head to pass under the lintel of the kitchen door.

Inside, standing with her back to him, she was untying her apron, and threw it over a chair before turning to him again.

'Oh, Ian.' Her lips tightened and her eyes glistened with tears.

'Oh, Ian, I just can't believe it. I just can't believe it.'

'Well, it's me right enough, Mother,' he said, and picking her up, hugged her and swung her round. As he set her down she wiped each eye with her palm and said, in tones which he knew so well that he could only raise his eyes to the ceiling and laugh, 'I'll just put the kettle on.'

Over tea she questioned him: Why had he not let them know? How did he come? How long was he staying? Was he well? But in her excitement she hardly listened to his answers and uncharacteristically never followed them up when they were evasive. He knew it would not be so easy when his father came in, but he was relieved nevertheless when his footstep was heard on the loose stones at the door. When John Archie MacRae entered it was clear that he had foreknowledge of his son's arrival. You never could do a thing here, thought Ian wryly, without the whole island knowing within a matter of hours.

Like most of the oldest islanders John Archie and Annie MacRae would normally speak Gaelic to each other in the home, and Ian had once used the language as comfortably as English. It was a measure of the strangeness between them that they addressed each other in English now.

'So it's yourself, Ian. Just stay where you are, don't get up.'

But Ian was on his feet and shaking his father by the hand, to the older man's obvious embarrassment. His eyes, brightly blue in the narrow, rutted, tanned face, looked aside quickly from his son's.

'How are you, Dad? You're looking great.'

'Ah, well, I'm not getting any younger, but there's some years in me yet.'

John Archie turned away to the shelf above the range and stood with his back to his wife and son, selecting a pipe from several standing in an ancient brown mug, and filling it with elaborate care.

'Are you here for a while?' he said, still without looking at Ian.

'Not really, Dad, just for a day or two. There's a conference in Bonn I'm going to, but I came a bit early to get the chance to see you.'

'Oh, aye. Well, you are welcome.'

And you are making me feel about as welcome as a downpour in the middle of haying, thought his son.

'Ian.' His mother was smoothing the tablecloth nervously, 'Will you have a photo of the children with you, maybe?'

'Och, I'm sorry, Mother. I should have done that.'

'I would love to see the two of them,' she said, disappointed. 'I've never seen their photo, just the one you sent us when Alec was a wee tot. He must be nearly twelve, now, I was thinking.'

'That's right. Not long till he goes into high school, and he's a grand volleyball player. He's in the first team.'

'And wee Jeannie, how old is she?'

'She's … nine, Mother.'

His voice was hesitant, but his mother did not notice.

'And who does she take after, Ian? Is she like yourself, or like Leela?'

'Her name's Leila, mother, not "Leela".'

He heard the irritation in his voice, and winced inwardly as his mother reacted to it, dropping her eyes sadly and answering in a small voice he remembered.

'I'm sorry, Ian, but I've just seen her name in your letters, like.'

'And there's been few enough of them,' said his father sharply, protectively.

The conversation, the first for so long, was not going at all the way Ian had planned. He paused, then used the technique which had served him so well in many boardrooms. He smiled at his mother and, standing up, put a hand on his father's shoulder.

'You're right, Dad, and it needs someone like you to give me a few home truths. Here, Dad, will you take me and show me what's been going on all this time? My mother has been telling me some of it, but there must have been a lot of changes. I see you've built a grand big barn.'

His father reacted as he knew he would to a show of interest in the croft.

'Aye, we got this grant two years ago, and Archie – you'll remember Archie MacPhail from Brodach – he gave me a hand putting it up. Do you want to come and have a look at it? You will need to get out of those fancy shoes.'

Equipped with black waders, turned down to knee height, and wearing a borrowed pullover covered with neat darns, the son walked again beside his father towards the steadings. Long and low, they had been built in stone by an earlier generation. Like the drystone walls still surrounding some of the smaller fields, the buildings had been laboriously constructed from boulders cleared from the grazing land or dragged on wooden sleds by horses from the shore. They had been built to last, and the regular replacement of the marram grass thatch had kept them warm and dry. Now the roofs were of tarred felt, and Ian remembered with distaste the annual task which had fallen to him of reproofing them with the help of a long-handled broom dipped in hot tar. It was a job he had hated.

The roofs were still in good order, but grass grew from between the stones of the four-foot-thick walls.

'I don't keep them just the way we used to,' said John Archie.

Is that supposed to make me feel guilty? thought Ian.

'I am just after the tarring,' his father went on. 'You get this stuff now, it does without the heating up.'

'You won't be needing these old steadings anymore, though, with the new barn,' Ian said.

It stood behind the steadings, twice as high and resplendent in corrugated sheeting, a monument to government subsidy.

'It is very handy, right enough, but you never know,' said John

Archie, with a sideways jerk of his chin. 'I doubt it will stand as long as the old ones. He was a dab hand at building, was my grandfather. But they are all getting these new things with the grants, so I thought I would give it a try. But I don't know at all.'

Ian remembered his father's pride and inherent reluctance to accept what he called handouts. Wary of a possible change of mood he shifted to another subject.

'How many sheep have you got now, Dad?'

'Well, I have maybe ninety gimmers, and I had fifty-one ewes and there are seventy-two lambs to go to the sales at the end of the month.'

'That sounds good. Have you been round them today, yet?'

'No,' said John Archie, 'I have not been round yet. Are you going to come?'

'I'd enjoy that, Dad.'

They walked mostly in silence across the uneven land keeping as far as possible to the ridges of high ground, a well-remembered route which ensured a view of every gulley and dip so that no animal was passed unspotted. Knowing this was always a slow round, Ian subdued his natural impatience, because he saw this time spent with his father as an investment.

A hare got up from its daytime hide in a clump of wild flags and lolloped away high-backed between the rocks to find another place where it could crouch undisturbed till night and grazing time came again. The collie dog that ran from side to side behind the two men, keeping low to the ground, ignored the hare in the urgent hope of being sent on a more exciting mission to find an errant member of the flock. Its white legs turned brick red from paddling through the peaty bog water, and its black coat was sleek in the sun. Small brown wheatears, flitting officiously from rock to rock, squeaked warnings of the dog's passing though surely aware from experience of its one-purpose mind.

The older man felt a disturbed pleasure in his son's company, at once familiar and unfamiliar, and though he was longing to talk to him he was too fearful of breaking the shell of acceptance with which the passage of time had covered the pain between them.

The row had been about a girl. She had been two years younger than Ian and their paths had barely crossed at the little island school in Torisay, forerunner of the bigger modern one in Balinbeag. Boys and girls mixed in class and avoided each other like infectious diseases afterwards. At the secondary stage, in adolescence, any mutual interest between a boy and a girl was instantly noted and those who indulged were subjected mercilessly to catcalls and jibes from their peers.

Ian, 'a young man with a bright future', Miss Louden had called him once, spent the term times during his A level years staying away with an aunt on the mainland. From there he had progressed to Glasgow University to read engineering. In the vacations at home he had studied, more or less assiduously, having neglected to do so during the term, and his father sensed regretfully his dwindling interest in the croft.

It was in August, just after Ian's finals, that the affair began. No one was unaware that Ian MacRae was 'carrying on' with Maggie Jamieson. He had stopped by the shop in Torisay to pick up some cigarettes, paid his money over to Maggie, who had worked at the till since she had left school, and as Calum MacQueen from Brodach put it, 'they hadn't looked back since.'

Calum was Maggie's father, not her real father, because she had been 'boarded out' with the MacQueen family as a small child. They had brought her up as one of their own. Calum had been a close friend of John Archie MacRae, and the ending of the friendship as a result of the whole business was one of the things which had deeply wounded Ian's father. The Saturday fishing trips in Calum's boat had been as regular as the tides themselves since the two men had been at school together. Both Calum and John Archie had been happy about the developing relationship between the two young people, and the thought that it might tie Ian more closely to the island had cheered his parents greatly.

So the end of it came as an appalling shock. There had been a 'shopping trip' to Glasgow when the pair had been observed sitting close and silent on the boat, away from the other passengers. There had been the return ferry journey two days later when Maggie was seen pale and weeping in the ladies' toilet by Jean MacBride, from Torisay Hotel (who was on her way home from her aunt's funeral in Stirling), and Ian had been seen drinking heavily at the bar.

All this was widely known within hours, because Jean, though no natural lover of humanity, nevertheless found endless satisfaction in passing on gathered information to her neighbours.

Two days later there had been a helicopter which had landed on the stretch of green machair just above the Brodach bog behind the MacQueens' house and wafted the unconscious Maggie off on a stretcher to the hospital in Inverness.

No one knew what words John Archie had used to his son, but his mother had repeated Ian's words to her most trusted friend, who had repeated it to the minister's wife, and so the whole island had heard it.

'Dad, no way were we going to have that baby. She didn't want it, and I didn't want it, and I paid for the whole thing myself. How could I know it would go wrong?'

The following morning Ian had again been on the boat, but this time alone. He had spoken to no one on the pier, and no one had been there to say goodbye to him. A letter from Springfield, Illinois, four months later, had assured his mother that he was 'fine' and would write again, which he did at increasingly long intervals, giving bare details of his movements and jobs. John Archie and Annie learned in time of his marriage, of the birth of his two children, of a move to the west coast. They knew of his changes of address, but not much more.

Annie had treasured his letters and read them many times before laying them in an old biscuit tin decorated with two pink-bowed kittens in a drawer of the kitchen dresser. The kittens guarded her most precious possessions – her mother's wedding ring; her father's medal from the war; Ian's birth certificate; the white envelope containing the certificates of all his exam results and a brown and crumbling sprig of heather, still held together by a faded bow of narrow, pale blue ribbon, which she had worn on her wedding day. The bundle of letters was very thin.

She had answered Ian's letters, on a pad of lined airmail paper kept in the same drawer for the purpose, but not with ease. She had never been good at expressing herself in writing and, because he gave her so little information on which to comment, she found she had trouble in filling the pages. All she could do was give him stilted information about events on the island, and as time went by it had become harder. She always wrote for his birthday, spending a long time reading the poems in the cards in the shop in Torisay before selecting the least unsuitable.

As the two men turned for home, having accounted for all the flock and tightened a sagging fence wire, they paused on the brow of a small hill, the father leaning with both hands on the horn handle of his long shepherd's crook.

'What a view,' said Ian, smiling, as his eyes roamed over the long uneven slope of rock and heather which fell away below them. On the greener land that levelled out into the narrow coastal plain, the sheep were scattered like daisies on the grass and crested lapwings strolled among them. Occasionally one of the birds rose into the air on its blunt-ended wings like a kite wafted sideways on an invisible string. Nearer by, groups of adolescent lambs, too big and too much trouble for their dams to fuss about, dashed in gangs from the tops of rocky mounds, bounding in stiff-legged exuberance.

Beyond the thirteen neat white houses of the township lay the sea of brochure blue. Far, far away, through a ghostly lavender haze, the mountains of the mainland were like wraiths of the imagination, a sure sign of continuing good weather.

'Aye,' said John Archie, 'it is a grand view. There is none better.'

Ian, sweating profusely, folded his legs and his heavy body subsided onto a lichen-yellowed rock. His father remained standing, still leaning on his stick, still gazing out to sea.

'It has been a long time, Ian,' he said.

'I know, Dad. Fifteen years next month.'

'Your mam, she was always looking for you.'

'Dad, it's a long way, halfway round the world. And you know I've been – well, I had to make some money, and when you've got something rolling you can't just walk out. I've always wanted to come. That's why I'm here now. Because I got the chance.'

'Aye. Well.'

There was a long pause. Somehow his father had always managed to make him feel at a disadvantage, thought Ian, irritated. It was never by what he said, but by what he left unsaid. He used his silences as other men used words, and silence is a hard argument to answer.

'Dad?'

John Archie looked down at him.

'What happened to her, Dad? Maggie Jamieson?'

Looking back at the sea, his father replied. 'She's in Aberdeen. She married an oil fellow.'

'Oh, that's great,' said Ian quickly. 'I just wanted to know she was all right.'

A pause, again. Then his father looked down at him, but he was lying back, a scrap of heather between his teeth, gazing with half-closed eyes into the milky blue of the sky, where high and invisible above them a lark twittered aimlessly.

'Dad,' he said, after a bit, 'I've been meaning to tell you and my mother: my marriage is finished.'

'Finished?'

'Yes, well, it wasn't right from the start. I knew pretty soon I'd made a mistake. But anyway, Leila left me a year ago. I got a divorce. She went off with an oil man too – there's a laugh for you!'

John Archie was not laughing.

'She went off? After twelve years being married?'

He was shaken.

'Well, it was never right, as I said,' said his son. 'We never really got on. She's just one of those people who can't recognise a good time when they're having it. She had everything you could want, and more. She had no idea what real life is about. Anyway, she's gone.'

'And your children? What about them?'

'Oh, I got the children, don't worry.' Ian laughed. 'I made sure of that. It was her that walked out on me, and I wasn't going to let her have the children. I got a woman in to help me.'

Then Ian rolled over on his side, and propped up on one elbow told his father he was planning to get married again, this was a really wonderful girl, he'd known her for a long time. She was great – real style – he wished his father could see her right now, he would just love her. They were going to have a really great time together. The faint American inflection in his voice became more noticeable as he spoke, and his face more animated.

He paused and waited for his father's reaction. It was not what he had expected.

'Ian, what has made you come back to the island now?'

Ian sat up.

'Dad, I wanted to tell you all this, obviously. And I wanted to see the two of you.'

'That is why you came back? To tell this to myself and your mother?'

'Why else?' said Ian uneasily.

His father did not reply to this. He lifted his cap and resettled it on his grey head.

'We'll be getting back. Your mother will be ready with our tea.'

So now he knew, thought Ian. So far, so good. But he didn't make it easy. At that moment, if he could have thought of any alternative to asking his parents for help, Ian would have taken it.

Later in the evening, it being Friday, Ian's father went to Torisay in his small pick-up van. He was not a great drinker, but it was his habit to meet his friends and neighbours once a week in the hotel bar and he hoped this week to see Neil MacNeill, better known as Neil the Pump, and ask him for a hand with some fencing.

Ian expected to be asked to go along too but was relieved when the invitation did not come. This would give him a chance to talk with his mother on her own.

They sat on either side of the range in the fading evening light, the woman with her head bent over some mending, the clock ticking on the smoke-brown mantel shelf. Why doesn't she put the light on? he thought. Nothing had changed, this careful frugality, this obsession with making things last. 'There's years of wear in that yet,' was the expression he remembered. What was the money for if not to make you more comfortable, to buy the things you needed, for Chrissake?

The kitchen was just as he remembered it. The walls had been repainted, perhaps a lighter shade of yellow, but the smoke from the range had put the dark patches back where they were before. There was still no refrigerator, just the grilled larder box outside where the milk and butter was kept cool by the wind. If the milk did go sour, she used it for making scones, so it wasn't wasted. The linoleum of the floor, whose pattern he could have drawn by heart, had a hole worn in it in front of the range. There was another in front of the sink, and each was disguised with a small plastic mat.

Surely they were not short of money? he wondered. The croft was a good one, and his father was still strong and fit. No, it was just that they had a low needs level and a habit of patient acceptance, unlike himself, who was made differently. Well, it took all sorts, luckily, and it was these very qualities and peculiarities of his parents he needed to draw on now. In future they would have no shortage of cash: he would see to that.

Then, carefully, with well-planned words, he brought up the subject he had travelled so far to talk about.

Ian had taken a room in the hotel, and he drove down to Torisay when his father returned, leaving his parents alone together. His mother, silent and disturbed, had made no effort to persuade him to stay in his old bedroom. He didn't mind.

Annie MacRae recounted their conversation to her husband late that night as they lay side by side under the sloping ceiling of their bedroom in the roof. The red pine tongue-and-groove slats had absorbed their quiet words for many years now, had heard expressions of joy and of sorrow, but only once before of such searing pain.

She told him, factually, almost without emotion, first Ian's proposition to her and then the details. She was determined to be fair and to say everything, just as Ian had expressed it. There were long pauses between her sentences. She repeated herself, and went back to things she had said earlier, adding to them.

She is spinning it out, John Archie thought. He could tell it helped her to delay the moment when he must comment, as if until then the whole thing might only be in her imagination. He let her run on for as long as she felt the need, himself dreading the next step.

'I just couldn't believe it at the start,' she said, 'when he told me. I just had this picture of the children, and him and Leila, in my mind all these years. And to hear now that they never got on … and then poor wee Jeannie. I don't know … the way he talks about them … and I always thought wee Jeannie would be so bonnie. Leila wanted to have the children, but she was the one to leave, so the judge was on Ian's side, her going off with another man and that. She wanted them all the same. But Ian says she wasn't fit to have them. But … I think it was only Alec he wanted.'

She gave a long shuddering sigh, and then went on.

'He had to promise they would both stay in the family – that he wouldn't put the wee lassie in a home. Poor wee thing … she has to have everything done for her, just like a baby. He says she doesn't … she isn't … he says her … her brain doesn't work at all … he told me the name of it, what's wrong with her, but I can't mind it now. It was a long name. The doctors say she'll not live more than a few years … then he's met this other girl. He told me about her, he says…'

Her husband nodded as he lay on his back, his eyes fixed on a knot in the bare sloping wood above him. She went on.

'He's just desperate to marry her, but she'll not take the wee lassie. She'll take Alec, but not wee Jeannie… He says it wouldn't be fair to ask her, with her being a young woman and that. She's not used with children, and Jeannie not being … well … it wouldn't be fair to ask her, he says.'

She paused.

After a little John Archie said, 'So he is asking you.'

'Aye, that's what he wants. He wants us to have her here. He says the court would accept that, so he thinks. Then he could get married.'

Another long pause. She seemed to have no more to say.

'What did you say to him?'

'What did I say to him? … I don't know what I said to him. What could I say to him?'

She made a low moaning sound that seemed to come from the

very depth of her being, a sound he had not heard since the night his son was born. He turned and put his hand on her shoulder as she lay with her thin back towards him. Soon she was silent again.

Then, 'He said he would pay. He offered us money. He's offering us *money...*'

She caught her breath in a long shuddering gasp and John Archie rose on his elbow beside her.

'Wheesht now, my lass, wheesht now.'

His hand didn't leave her shoulder and his voice caressed her gently. After many minutes he felt her become still again, as her racking, soundless sobs gradually subsided. He lay down again beside her and, eventually, she slept.

Mentally, Ian's father went through agony that night. He knew his wife had in effect asked him to make the decision as to what they should do, and he knew also that as on that previous occasion she was so emotionally shaken she could not cope with the situation herself.

Fifteen years earlier she had been distraught, not so much because of what her son had made his girlfriend go through as that he had, as she put it, 'got rid of' her grandchild. It was as if the child had been torn from her own body and her pain, with the additional refinement that it was her beloved son who had caused it, had been distressing to watch and live with. Ian's departure and his lack of farewells had been a further twist of the knife.

John Archie and Annie were a close and well-matched couple, but they never used many words in communication with each other, and it was not in the nature of either to 'talk things through'. They had been brought up to be patient and stoic in adversity, and when John Archie longed to help and comfort his wife he found he had no aptitude for it. He had only been able to get on with the work of the croft, to watch and to wait. Years had passed before he felt she had put the whole thing behind her and become more like the partner and companion he had once known.

Now Annie again had the chance, dismissed long ago as something which would never happen, of caring for her son's child. But it was to be a damaged child, an unwanted child, and to that had been added the torturing insult of an offer of payment for her pains.

In the quiet of the night John Archie faced the options. If they accepted Ian's proposition, as Annie's husband he would have to endure more years of the loneliness he knew would be his lot while his wife cared night and day for a mentally and physically disabled child. It would drain her in both mind and body, and the work on the croft would be left entirely to him. And since Annie would inevitably come to love the child, it would all end in tragic bereavement. He had no idea what this would do to her, but he dreaded the possibility that this time he might never totally reclaim her.

If he said 'yes' in the morning, and released his incurably selfish son to the freedom of his new marriage, it would give his wife the grandchild she craved, but it would mean condemning her to a servitude which could only end in sorrow.

Or he could say 'no', and maintain, on the face of it at least, the pattern of life he had known for so many years. It would estrange still further, possibly for ever, the son he had once loved, and whom Annie loved still. Would she ever forgive him for that? How long would it be until he knew? And could he himself stand the strain while he waited to see if she recovered from this final blow? She would not leave him, he knew that, but their lives could become indescribably bleak.

He turned the possibilities over in his mind until he was so confused and tired that his eyes, dry for half a century, ached for the relief of tears. He wanted to touch his wife for the consolation of company but feared to wake her.

As dawn threw the mainland hills into dark silhouette, he quietly left the bed and, pulling back the faded curtains from the dormer window, stood for a long while looking out. In front of him, sleeping under a light layer of mist, lay the land he had tended since boyhood, land he had worried over, worked at, fed, and cared for till it was as much a part of him as if he were rooted into it, land he had once hoped to pass on to his son. He pondered, not for the first time, whether the land was there to feed the people, or were the people there to care for the land. The need was mutual – each would dwindle away without the other. There was a potential sermon in that, one the minister had not yet thought of. What would the minister think of his dilemma, or would he know at once which was the 'right' thing to do?

A luminous glow was spreading up the sky and its reflection lit the sloping ceiling above the bed. John Archie turned and looked at his wife as she lay, much younger in her sleep than when she was up and working. There was no care now in her face.

He remembered how Ian's offer of money had hurt her so greatly and his anger rose within him. It was intolerable that Ian should understand his mother so little. But he, Ian's father, understood her and suddenly he knew he had enough strength and love for her to cope with any result of his decision.

He made it then, not the decision he felt to be morally right, but the one his instinct told him was right. Having made it, he felt as if a crushing burden had been lifted from him. As he got back into bed his wife stirred and reached out for his hand, and he slept at last.

And so the big man found himself once again at the rail of the ferry boat, once again sailing away from the island, but this time he stood facing the line of rocky hills which was all that remained to be seen of his native shore before it sank below the horizon. If the rage seething in his heart had been transmutable through his eyes the whole island would surely have leapt into the air like a volcanic explosion.

When his father had called him inside that morning and told him he should go home and care for his own stricken child his anger had flared at once. He had been certain his mother would conform to his wishes and at once realised his father was responsible for this refusal. He had made the mistake of trying to change John Archie's mind by shaming him into agreement. 'She's your granddaughter, Dad, and you can give her a better life than I can. There'll be no lack of funds.'

The result shook him. For once there had been no expressive silence but an eloquence that had left the son speechless. The expressions of scorn had seared into him and burned as on raw flesh. The final words still rang in his head.

'Your girlfriend doesn't want her, and you don't want her, but by God, Ian, you'll not give me money to perform your abortion for you. You'll not buy yourself out of this one.'

There was no more to be said, and Ian left without seeing his mother. He never came back.

The first few days were bad, as they had to be, and John Archie worked long hours, rising early and staying out till dark had fallen. However, his wife was quiet and composed when he saw her, and although he was aware that she slept lightly she showed little sign of distress. After a few weeks he began to realise a new closeness was developing between them, fostered by Annie. She was going out of her way to spend more time with him in the fields and around the steadings than she ever had since they were newly married. He hardly knew what to make of it, and only very slowly came to the conclusion that not only was this change a lasting one, but it was a direct result of the decision he had taken in relation to Ian: Annie had stopped mourning. She was actually looking only towards John Archie and the croft for the first time since Ian had gone to America fifteen years before. She seemed to have decided and accepted that the episode which Ian represented in their lives was finally over.

Only now that she was returning to his side did John Archie realise how far away she had been. He was overwhelmed by this surprising and happy outcome of their tragedy. All he had hoped for was survival.

A year or so later, a letter arrived at the croft house, an airmail letter which had 'interesting' written all over it, thought Archie the Post. For one thing, it had American stamps on it, which he hoped he might claim later for his small philatelist son. For another, the only writing on the envelope beyond 'Mr J. A. MacRae, crofter', was the name of the island, and 'Scotland, U.K.' But though he was politely thanked, and offered a cup of tea, which he accepted, hoping this might enable him to be present at the opening, he learned nothing of the letter's contents.

It lay on the dresser until John Archie and Annie were together in the evening; then Annie opened it and read it aloud.

It was from Leila, and it was not long. It related how Ian's attempts to get his daughter into a home had been reported to the divorce court judge, and how a renewed application from herself, the child's mother, for custody of both children had been granted.

The letter ended, 'Jeannie is not well, but I know she knows me, and this is a real consolation. I am so happy to have her with me again. When it is all over, and the doctor says it will not be long now, Jamie and I want to take a trip, the honeymoon we never had.

'I hope I can say this in a way that will give no offence. We are going to bring young Alec to Europe with us, and we would be so proud to introduce you to your grandson. Please, will you write and say if this would be acceptable.'

The grandfather got to his feet and took his pipe and tobacco pouch down from the mantel shelf. He stood with his back to his wife as he stuffed it with tobacco. He had some trouble in lighting it, which gave him a few minutes' respite and gave her a chance to get rid of the tears that were brimming in her eyes.

Soon he spoke. 'Well, Annie love, what do you say? I think that would be acceptable.'

NEIL

2010s

'Grand weather,' said Neil, with a sideways jerk of his chin. He was sitting on the bench by the front door of his cottage, his pipe between his teeth, working at the netting of an old wood-framed lobster creel gripped between his knees.

The two cyclists paused gratefully at his greeting. Their backpacks were heavy, and the evening, though it was late September, was hot. There was a picture postcard quality about the whitewashed cottage, with its tarred felt roof, sitting tucked in at the side of the road just before the top of the rise. They were happy to stop in front of it. They had dismounted some way back to push their mountain bicycles, which were laden with bags over the back wheels.

'Isn't it lovely? And what a view!' said the girl, wiping the shine from her forehead with the back of her hand. She was small, and pale, with ash blonde hair and surprisingly muscular legs.

Her accent made Neil look at her again and take his pipe out of his mouth. He pushed his cap up a little from his eyes. It was of a tweed whose colours had years ago merged into one. It never left his head until he rolled into bed at night.

'You'll be from England, then,' he said.

'That's right,' said her companion, a young man with a plethora of photographic equipment hanging round his neck, thudding against his stomach as he moved. 'We're from South of the Border, what you people refer to as Sassenachs. Do you mind if we stop here a minute or two? And, er, *cia mar a tha thu?*' He gave a slightly self-conscious laugh. His prominent Adam's apple bobbed up and down as he spoke.

'*Tha gu math,*' Neil answered the greeting in Gaelic and continued in English. 'No, no, I do not mind at all. Just you sit yourselves down and have a good rest. It is a warm day, right enough.'

He moved along the bench to make room for them. They propped their bicycles against the end wall of the cottage and slid their packs from their shoulders. Flopping down beside Neil, the young man shook the front of his shirt and pushed his rolled-up sleeves a little higher up his freckled forearms. He took off his spectacles and wiped the sweat from the lenses with a green spotted handkerchief.

'I don't think we came properly equipped for this expedition,' he said ruefully. 'By rights you should be having the tail end of the equinoctial gales.'

'Is that so?' Neil surveyed him with an expression of deep interest.

Once again he twitched his cap back, as if to see more clearly. In fact very little escaped the brilliantly blue eyes, which looked young in the worn skin of his old man's face.

'The Scottish Tourist Board gave us very inaccurate information about the weather, I'm afraid, which certainly wasn't helpful.'

'Is that so? Well, maybe they did not know themselves. And are you on a long trip?'

'Just a week,' said the young man. 'It's a working holiday, really. I am in the Department of Social Anthropology at Sussex, and I am completing my thesis on Gaelic Culture. I've really dealt with the Hebridean section already, but I felt that a visit to one or two of the islands would help me add certain flavours to the final draft.'

'Well, well…' said the old man. 'This will be your first visit to the island, then?'

'That's right,' said the girl eagerly, leaning forward from her seat and smiling past the young man into Neil's face, 'and Peter has collected such a lot of material already, just in one day. We have been staying in the little hotel down in Torisay, and we met some wonderful characters.'

'Aye. Well, there's a fair number of folk in Torisay. It is a busy place.'

Neil was aware of the bikers exchanging glances before the young man spoke again.

'Torisay is the largest conglomeration, I think. Forty-two people in the township – isn't that what you call the hamlets?'

'Oh, so you know a lot about the island, then?'

The young man smiled and raised a forefinger.

'That's my job. But you don't know our names. Peter Backshall, from Hemel Hempstead, and this is my fiancée, Linda.'

Neil accepted his outstretched hand.

'My name,' he said, 'is Neil Archibald MacBride, and I am very pleased to meet you, Mr Backshall. And you too, Miss er – er…'

'Ribble, but soon I'll be Backshall,' she giggled, 'but just Linda, really, Hi!'

Leaning forward, Neil stretched across and shook her hand as well.

'May I offer you both my congratulations and wish you great happiness,' he said formally. 'Now, I hope you will be taking a cup of tea. I am just after putting the kettle on for myself.'

'Oh, that would be wonderful,' said Linda. 'I think it would save my life.'

'Thank you, if it's not too much trouble,' said Peter.

Neil edged the creel away with his foot, then leaning well forward and pushing himself up by the backs of his fingers on the bench, he rose laboriously to his feet.

'Can I give you a hand, Mr – um – do let me help you make the tea.'

'No, no,' he motioned her down. 'Don't stir yourself. I can manage fine once I'm on my feet. I get a touch of the rheumatics every now and then, but it is not much.'

He moved through the porch door and out of sight. He looked older standing up, they thought, a bent figure in his paint-dappled blue dungarees.

Linda leant back against the sun-warmed wall and shut her eyes.

'Oh dear,' she said, 'I have forgotten his name already. Isn't he perfect, though? Real, old-world courtesy, and that wonderful accent. He understood your Gaelic too.'

'MacBride,' said Peter. 'It's a very common name in this part of the Hebrides – affiliated to the Clan MacDonald. They're very inbred, especially in these smaller islands. Now, this is very interesting. In these primitive societies the offering of food and drink to visitors is almost a ritual, and must never be refused. It would be a major insult to say no.'

'Well, I'm gasping, anyway. I wasn't going to say no.'

She stuck her tongue out and panted. Her companion did not smile.

'Now, Linda, this is a great opportunity to talk to one of them informally like this, and we mustn't waste it. I want you to help me draw him out, but gently.'

The young man dropped his voice a little, aware of the half-open window at his shoulder.

'See if we can get him on to folk tales. Some of these old fellows are full of them if you can once get them going. It's a pity we can't prime him with a drop of whisky. That would do the trick.'

After some minutes, Neil emerged through the open doorway carrying a tin tray with teapot, cups and saucers, milk, and a sugar bowl. In the centre of it all was a bowl covered by a plate on which lay two spoons.

'Mr Backshall, would you be so good as to bring that wee table out the porch?'

Peter placed the table in front of the bench and the tray was placed on it.

'Would you like me to pour, Mr MacBride?' asked Linda.

'No, indeed, that would not do at all. It is for me to do the honours on the occasion of your visit.'

You see? said Peter's expression, as Linda sat back.

When they all had a cup of tea in their hands Neil raised his to the height of his eyes, looked at his visitors seriously and spoke several unintelligible words.

Then he took a sip of his tea.

'May I ask what you just said, Mr MacBride?' asked Peter. 'My Gaelic is rather basic, I'm afraid.'

'It is a customary greeting that we make when a visitor is about to partake of our simple fare. It expresses a wish that he may never forget his visit.'

'I am sure we never will,' said Linda with enthusiasm, leaning forward to smile at Neil. 'It is a privilege just to sit here and look at your lovely view.'

From its position near the top of the hill the cottage commanded a fine panorama westwards, where the road sloped away towards the sea and round the lower shoulder of a more craggy hill a mile or so further on. Shading her eyes from the sun, which was now halfway down the sky, Linda looked across the uninhabited stretch of rock-strewn land, an occasional sheep the only sign of life, and thought what a lonely place this must be in the winter, despite the beauty now.

'And now,' said Neil, 'you will do my humble roof the honour of sharing between you this bowl of carragheen.'

He lifted the plate.

'Goodness, what is that?' said Linda, looking with assumed interest and barely concealed revulsion as a bowl of slightly quivering opaque white jelly was held before them.

'It is the carragheen,' said Neil in tones of surprise. 'I am sure you must know it, Mr Backshall, from your studies.'

'Oh yes, of course, I have heard of it, but never actually seen it, I mean, not actually in edible form. It – it is made from some kind of seaweed, isn't that right?'

'It is drawn,' said Neil, 'from the pure essence of the young dark carragheen. Only at the lowest spring tide will the ocean draw back to reveal this life-giving plant, and not always then. They used to say that only the purest young girls could find the true weed. I would not know about that, but I do know that we treasure it and always have some ready for an honoured visitor. It is cooked, as you will know, Mr Backshall, after many weeks of turning and drying in the sun. It is on hand, then, to prepare when visitors are due. It takes just an hour or two to set.'

'I believe it has medicinal qualities?' said Peter.

'It has many qualities,' said Neil, 'and some would call them medicinal. Our forefathers would not have gone into battle without it, nor their womenfolk gone into labour without its protection. It has other properties, too, that I would not be mentioning in front of the young lady.'

But Linda was not listening.

'Mr MacBride,' she said hesitantly, 'this may be a silly thing to ask, but did you know we were coming? I mean, having the carragheen ready and – well...'

Neil picked up his pipe from the bench beside him. It had gone out, so he tapped the burnt tobacco out onto the ground. Then he lifted his head and, with his eyes on the horizon, said,

'Miss Ribble, there is nothing silly in your question. I can only say to you that your arrival was not unexpected.'

Linda pushed a finger into Peter's thigh, and he gave her a slight warning shake of his head.

'Well,' said Neil, 'please, will you help yourselves, now, as you would in your own house.'

Each with a spoon tasted the carragheen jelly.

'It is very interesting,' said Peter after a pause during which he had made little wet sounds with his lips, his eyes distantly focused. 'Unusual. Very good, really. Amazing how firmly it sets.'

'Mm,' said Linda. 'Fascinating.'

She stared into the bowl. Following Peter's example she took some more on the tip of her spoon. Neil watched them seriously as he drank his tea. He uttered a few more words in Gaelic and translated them.

'I am saying that you are welcome to it, from the bottom of my heart. May it do you both good.'

Soon Linda, with a muffled 'excuse me', got to her feet and went round the corner of the house. After a few minutes she came back.

'Just getting a handkerchief,' she said, smiling apologetically. She shook her head to Neil's offer of more carragheen.

When Peter had nearly emptied the bowl he pushed it slightly away and said, 'Are there many people on the island with the Sight, Mr MacBride?'

As usual, Neil paused for thought before speaking.

'It would be hard to tell,' he replied. 'It is not a thing you would find people talking about.'

He then very obviously changed the subject.

'So you have been staying at the hotel? You will not have to be leaving it very late to get back. The dark falls very quickly at this time of the year, and you have a few miles to go.'

'Oh no, we are not heading back tonight. We plan to get rooms down at this end, near Baideanach, I think it is called.'

Neil paused in the lighting of his pipe and looked at Peter.

'And where would you be thinking of staying down that way, if you do not mind my enquiring?'

'Not at all. Miss MacEachern, her name is – I am not quite sure how it is pronounced. She has a card up in the shop in Torisay.'

Neil stared at him for some seconds, and then turned his head towards the distant craggy hill.

'Moraig MacEachern,' they heard him mutter, and then some words in Gaelic.

'You sound surprised,' said Peter. 'Do you know Miss MacEachern?'

'Aye,' Neil's reply sounded reluctant. 'Everybody knows Moraig MacEachern, in a manner of speaking.'

'Does she have a lot of visitors?'

'Visitors, is it? Well, it depends on what you mean by visitors.'

The old man was no longer meeting their eyes. He brushed invisible dust from the knee of his overalls with the back of big blunt-ended fingers.

'Mr MacBride,' said Peter, 'you are being very mysterious. I don't want to ask you to tell tales on your neighbours, but is it a good place to stay the night? Just bed and breakfast, we want.'

There was a long pause as the old man fiddled with the black tobacco pouch on the bench beside him, his eyes sweeping the horizon. At last he turned to look at them and they were both struck by the change in his expression. His eyes still seemed to be focused on some point far beyond them, and his jaw was rigid as he spoke, in a lower tone than before.

'I would not spend a night under that roof if you were to give me all the gold in this world.'

'Good heavens, what's wrong with the place?' said Peter, leaning forward, pushing his glasses up his nose with his forefinger.

Another pause, as Neil thought deeply.

'You may be right, Mr Backshall, when you say that it is the place that is wrong. It may be that if Moraig MacEachern had never gone there at all she would have been no different from anybody else. But then, no ordinary person would have stayed, as she did, when they once knew what was going on. Unless … unless she was unable to leave. I don't know at all.'

Again he said, 'I don't know at all…'

His voice was dreamy, as if he were thinking aloud and had forgotten his audience. Linda moved a little closer to Peter and slipped her hand under his arm. He squeezed it against his side and said, 'I think I will have to ask you to tell us more, Mr MacBride. We will be very discreet about it; you should know that. I mean, we won't repeat a word of what you tell us.'

Once again Neil MacBride turned his head towards the hill whose jagged shape was darkening against the evening sky. After another thoughtful pause he began.

'I am an old man now, but I was at school with Moraig MacEachern, here on the island. She was a year or two older than me. She was a nice enough girl, but very quiet. She lived with her mother – there was just herself in the family, and her mother was a widow. Then she died, the mother, and there was no one to look after the lassie but a distant relative of her father's who lived in the house in at the back of yon hill. She was what they called a recluse.'

He pronounced the word to rhyme with choose.

'Now, she was one they say had the Sight, but nobody knew much about her. She kept herself to herself and nobody saw her go in or out. There was nobody to see her, anyway – there's nobody lives near that house. There were stories about her, about strange comings and goings and cries in the night. She had a reputation, you might say, and folk were nervous of the place, so they kept away. She had a cow, and that kind of thing, so she wanted for nothing that would bring her to the village. All the same, she knew that the lassie was an orphan, though nobody knows who told her, and she applied to have her, and she got her, being a relative.

'And that was the last any of us saw of Moraig MacEachern for a good many years. She stopped coming to the school. We all left at fourteen in those days, and she must have been nearly that. We heard the teacher called in one day to see her when she was down by, and got the door slammed in her face, so she didn't try again.

'That was nearly sixty years ago. I mind when I was a young man we used to go courting up on the hill there. Sitting up on the rocks there was a grand view and nobody else in sight. Except for those two, the old one and the young one. Times you would see them, always bent over, filling their aprons or their bags. We never could tell what kind of thing they were gathering, weed, maybe, from the shore, and whelks. But on the sand dunes it would be the snails there, that live in the tufts of the marram grass. Very strange they are, those snails, Mr Backshall. They move on a trail of slime, but they never pick up the sand. And the big black slugs, three inches long, they can be, when they're moving, evil things…

'We could never do more than guess what they were up to, the two women. As soon as they knew we were there, and they could always tell, however well we were hidden, they would stop and go back into the house. It is one of the old ones, a black house with deep, deep windows and a turf roof with marram thatch. It is just the same now. I mind one day we were not so far up the hill, and the wind was blowing their way, and the lassie I was with cried out to them.

'"Hallo, Moraig," she called.

'And Moraig turned her head away, but the old one, she shook her fist at us, and pointed at us with her finger, and I'm telling you we ran and never looked back.

'Well,' said Neil MacBride, straightening his back in a long stretch and then resuming his position with his elbows on his knees and his big hands clasped between them. His cap was down, low on his brow. He glanced at the couple beside him and, seeing he had their full attention, he continued.

'That was the way of it for a long time. And then, maybe ten years after that, the old woman died. Now I only heard this I'm going to tell you, so I don't know the truth of it. But I knew the doctor, Dr Wynn it was then, and he was not a fanciful man.

'It seems he was going by on the road in his wee motor car, and when he got to the place where the track comes in from behind the hill the engine stopped, just like that. And he got out, and cranked the handle, and nothing happened, and he had plenty of petrol and everything. And he was just standing there, wondering what he should do. And then all of a sudden he felt that he was being called, not called so you would hear it, but drawn, drawn down the wee path that led over the rocks and through the bog to where the old house stood under the hill where the two women lived.

'He told the minister later that he could not for the life of him have resisted that call. He just found himself going down the path before he had even spoken with his feet. And when he got to the house, she was standing there in the doorway, the lassie, as if she was waiting for him. And her hair was wild, and her eyes were wild, and there was a kind of look of triumph about her, so he told me.

'And she said to him, with a funny kind of smile, "Moraig is dead."

'And the doctor knew who she was, so he said, "What are you saying, now, Moraig? Shall I take a look?"

'And she signed to him to come in, and it was so dark in there that he could see very little, and he looked around and then he saw her lying there in the gloom, the old woman. And the lassie lit a candle and held it up high. And he looked at the body, and she had fresh tangle weed lying over her, and her eyes, they were covered with two limpet shells. Not empty ones, live ones.

'And the lassie was just standing there with this funny wee smile, saying nothing. Well, the doctor knew the old woman must have been about ninety, so he was not concerned with the cause of death or anything like that. So he said, "Now you can leave it all to me, Moraig. I will get everything arranged. You had better come away now, and you can stay with one of the neighbours."

'And then, he said, she gave him a look that fair froze the marrow in his bones.

'"You leave me be," she said, "Moraig is dead."

'And her eyes were as cold as the stones on the shore. And the doctor, he didn't know what to say, so he said, "Can you tell me her full name, Moraig, for the certificate like?"

'And then the lassie laughed, and said, "Any name, it's all the same. You can call her Moraig, for Moraig is dead."

'And she laughed, and went on laughing, and her laugh was horrible, like the sound of a knife scraping on stone.

'And that was enough for the doctor, and he was off just as quick as he could get out the door, and up the path, and he was in such a hurry that it wasn't till later on that he realised that the engine of his motor started at the first try.

'So they came and took the body away, but Moraig MacEachern never came to the burial. Well, nobody did, just those that had to. And there was no gathering afterwards. At least, not in the village.

'Now,' said Neil, 'this is another thing I don't know for sure, but I might as well tell you. Well, on the night of the burial there was a storm and a great howling wind that lashed the island with huge waves. Oh, I mind that night well, for we nearly lost the roof of our own house, that was thatch in those days. But there was a man, he is passed away now, Donald MacAlister from down by. Donald Dhu they used to call him, dark Donald, for his hair. He lived in Cean Bodha, not more than a mile from the hill. And his wife was expecting, and, with all the thunder and lightning and that, she went into labour. And Donald set off to look for the midwife, who was living at that time up by Baideanach. And he took a short cut over the hill to get there quicker.

'And this is what he said, Donald Dhu, though I didn't hear it from him myself. When he was still up the hill a way he heard strange sounds, like mouth music, and he looked and he saw Moraig MacEachern's house all lit up in a halo of light, flickering, blue, and there was an eerie sound like the wailing of seals on the rocks and laughing and groaning all mixed together. And he said it sounded like some kind of celebration, but it was horrible to the ears. And he said the house was full of it, and full of those making the sound. And he stood there, did Donald Dhu, and he could not take his eyes from it, and he was forgetting where he was going. And the strange thing was it seemed to him that the sea was lapping right up to the walls of the house, but it could have been a trick of the light, the house being a good quarter of a mile from the shore. But that was the way it looked.

'And then, just like that, the noise ceased, and as he watched he saw that this strange light seemed to be pouring out of the house, out of the windows, out of the door and rolling up the hill towards him in a long stream, and it was hiss-ssing as it came.

'Well, he ran, and he was near dead with fright when he reached the midwife's. And she gave him a dram and put him in her own bed and went off on her bicycle in all that wind and delivered the baby with no trouble at all. And not a thing did she see on the road.'

There was a long silence and Peter cleared his throat. His

Adam's apple leapt up and down as he swallowed. But Neil had not finished. He sat up and pushed the peak of his cap slightly higher.

'Moraig MacEachern is an old woman now, well up in years, anyhow. She has been alone there all this time. She never goes far, and nobody sees her. The minister went to call when he first came to the island, but he never tried again. There's stories told, though, about the strange cries in the night, and sea creatures moving on the land. They say the sun never shines on the house – there's always a dark cloud over it, always a dark cloud…'

Neil's voice faded away again.

The sun was sinking and a chill breeze was coming in from the sea. The black mass off the hill seemed larger as it loomed starkly against the orange and purple sky.

When Peter spoke, his voice seemed thinner than before.

'But the card we saw up in the shop, what does that mean?'

'Well, now,' said Neil, 'I did not know about the card. I heard some talk, right enough that she was seen in Torisay a week or two ago, but you cannot always credit what folk say. Aye, and there was a man last week asking for Miss MacEachern's house. But he never stayed there – I know, because my daughter said he was looking for a room very late down by Cean Bodha. Maybe he got the same treatment as the minster.'

'But why advertise for lodgers just to turn them away?' said Peter. 'It doesn't make sense.'

'Well, I do not know if I should be saying this,' said Neil, 'but it may not be a man she is waiting for. She went there as a lassie when the old woman was nearing the end of her days. Maybe it is a lassie she is needing now.'

Linda was leaning forward with her eyes fastened on his face. He looked at her briefly, and then away again. The same tense look was in his features that they had seen earlier.

'There is strange goings on behind the hill there,' he said

musingly. 'Even the beasts know it. You'll not find a sheep or a bullock will graze on the hill after sunset, and the machair grows long near the house, and full of thistles.'

As he spoke, a light pattering sound they had heard turned into a small cluster of sheep trotting along the tarmac, coming over the rise from the right. The leading ewe stopped and stared for a moment at the three seated figures in front of the cottage, and then trotted on towards Torisay, followed by her little pack.

Neil watched as they went off down the long slope, then he continued.

'There is a wee lochan close behind the MacEachern house where the mallard and the teal and the greylag geese feed, but they will not one of them stay after the sun goes down. The birds and the beasts, they know more than we do.'

A long skein of wild geese was coming towards them out of the sunset and their sad klaxon cry seemed to sound a warning to the listeners below, who watched in silence as they passed overhead.

'They know,' repeated Neil, 'they know.'

'Oh, Peter,' said Linda, hugging the young man's arm and looking anxiously up at his face. She whispered something to him.

'It's all right, dear,' he said, patting her hand. 'Well, I want to thank you, Mr MacBride, for your hospitality and, er, all you've told us. It has been really interesting. Actually, I think perhaps with the boat leaving so early we would be better spending another night at the hotel in Torisay. I am sure Mr Bell will still have room. I'd like to take some photos there in the morning too. So, well, I think we'll be on our way.'

Linda was on her bicycle and away down the slope before Peter had his backpack properly adjusted, but with a wave of his hand he was soon peddling hard to catch her up.

Neil leaned back against the wall, watching their dwindling figures. He pushed his cap well back and slowly shook his head.

A car came over the brow and pulled up on the grass at the end of the cottage. A cheerful woman of about forty-five got out and greeted him. She carried a bundle of exercise books and children's drawings.

'I'm sorry I'm so late, Dad. I got held up after school, and then I had a few things to do on the way home. I'll get you your tea.'

'I had a cup in my hand a wee while ago,' said Neil, 'but I could do with a bite now.'

'You've had visitors, I see – who was that? And – I don't believe it? You've finished that carragheen I made you. Well done! What took you, Dad? I thought you couldn't stand it, you said?'

'No, that's the truth of it,' he said, rubbing his chin. 'But these two trippers, they took a fancy to it. Who was I to refuse them? Don't make any more, Jenny, because I can't eat the stuff.'

'Well,' said his daughter, smiling. 'I know it tastes horrible, but they do say it eases the rheumatics. It's full of iron. But don't worry – I'll not bother you with it any more. Who were these two, anyway?'

'Oh, Jenny,' said Neil, grinning back, 'they were a couple of innocents abroad, looking for local colour. So I gave them some.'

'What have you been up to, Dad?' Jenny stood in front of him with her hands on her hips. 'I can tell by that look on your face you've been enjoying yourself!'

'Oh … aye. They were planning to stay the night at Moraig MacEachern's.'

'Goodness,' she said. 'I hope you never sent them on down there. You know very well she's away at Jessie Lamont's wedding in Glasgow, and she won't be back for a week. That's what held me up – I promised to feed her hens for her, and she phoned this morning to say she had left her TV plugged in. Oh, my,' she clapped her hand to her mouth, 'it's my fault, then! She asked me to take her card down in the shop, and I clean forgot. Oh, goodness me, were they walking, those people? I hope you told them not to go on down to Moraig's.'

'Oh, aye,' said Neil, 'I told them right enough. They are away back to Torisay on their wee pedal bikes. I told them, never you worry.'

Jenny went into the cottage and came out with a whisky bottle and two glasses.

'Shall we have a dram, Dad? I could just do with one myself.'

She lifted her glass and gazed at the dying sun through the golden clarity of the liquid. Then she looked at her father and smiled.

'*Slàinte*!' she said.

He winked at her.

'Mud in your eye, Jenny.'

Island

I have a house in the Hebrides,
but it's never been really mine:
it belongs to the gulls that cry above
the rippled sands of the bay I love
and over the leaping wave-tops skim the far horizon line.

The house belongs to the rocks that steer
between their fortress walls
the grasping surge of a rising sea,
the boundless force that's always free
to choose on a stormy winter tide which building stands or falls.

It belongs to the night and the watching stars,
to the moon-path down the bay;
to the hungry wind that rattles roans
and licks the eaves with eerie moans;
to the rain that stings its naked face and turns the white skin grey.

It belongs to the singing, soughing seals
who bask on the rocks offshore,
and when the bay is full and wide
will hang like bells in the swaying tide
wondering with their soft brown eyes what humans can be for.

It belongs to the brooding eider duck
that plucks its own breast feather,
its gossamer down for the simple nest

that's fitter far for an angel's rest
than for a clutch of grey-green eggs in a craggy cleft in the heather.

This house belonged for a time to those
who worked reluctant land;
with calloused hands and aching bones,
they built its walls with the stubborn stones
they wrested from the moor above, and driftwood dragged
    from the sand.

Who owned the house when they were gone
but the birds that knew it most?
The soaring snipe with its drumming fall,
the wagtails, wheatears, whimbrels, all
have a greater claim to the house by the sea than I could ever boast.

I love this house as a silhouette
against the sunset glow;
I love it on a sparkling night
beneath the comets' fiery flight,
But I love it best when its sunlit face smiles down on the bay below.

I have a house in the Hebrides
and it felt like mine alone,
while the walls absorbed my joy and tears,
with tenderness, a few brief years;
But others soon will have the house, to love, but never own.

Acknowledgements

I shall always be grateful to my good friend, the artist Maggie Redfern, who first came to the Hebrides with me in 1958 and who drew the illustrations for this book. And I am equally grateful to Sam and Alice Carter, whose generous help and encouragement made the book happen.

About the Author

ALICE RENTON spent three months camping on a Hebridean island as a girl, and so began a long love affair with the islands. Brought up in Scotland, where three of her children and most of the rest of her family live, she migrated to England when she married and has lived ever since on the South Downs. Holidays every year are spent in the Hebrides.

Printed in Great Britain
by Amazon

43038173R10101